SUBJECT 9

SUBJECT 9

BRAD SHPRINTZ

Bradley Shprintz

First Printing, 2022

To the person reading this dedication, you are the other half of the dream! Thank you.

Contents

Part 1

Chapter 1

THE CALL

The day started grey, having a melancholy affair with Brand's state of mind. The grey reminded him of Philly, except there that was usual weather. Here in Sarasota, Florida, it was uncharacteristic, feeling unacceptable. Maybe that's why he was grumpier than he wanted to be with the call that had just transpired.

Hector had a good heart but always wanted easy money. Brand played the call back in his head, something he did often, being his own critic.

Hector had said, "Bro, it's easy money. Why you being like this?"

Brand had replied, "It's not my thing."

But Hector was not taking no, "Bro, I make a hundred and twenty and you twelve hundred, you know I need the money."

Brand could hear the pleading and desperation in Hector's voice. While knowing it was true, still said, "I'll do it for six hours for the full twelve hundred with no surprises. I'll be packing and won't hesitate. No cameras on me and only cash. That's the deal."

Hector was now getting angry, "Bubba's not going to do it. You're messing it up for us both."

Brand could care less, "Call me back if it's on, and can it be the week after?"

Hector was adamant on the last point, "Bro, it *has* to be on the 27th." Okay, Brand said, and that had been that.

Brand Wright was an average build with a height of 5 feet 10 inches, olive complexion, being neither fat nor thin. Most would say he looked younger than his age. The only feature that was distinctive was that at 63, he still had his hair, which was brown with very little grey near his ears and his eyes. They were a greyish blue that had a steel look to them. They had a cold look of fire that would set upon you, hypnotizing the subject with a lie detector's judgment of their soul. His eyes created a presence that gave him power.

Brand lived on a ten-acre spread that belonged to his farmer friends, Roy and Sarah. He had a 37-foot fifth-wheel trailer with four slides. Water was achieved through a filtered well, and the grey and dark went straight to the septic tank. With a modified 50 circuit electrical connection and a satellite dish, he had everything he needed.

The back of the trailer was angled to Roy and Sarah's home, sort of forming an L. His front view was beautiful. His "pittie" or pit bull to those who don't own one, was the most loving dog on the planet. She lived for making sure everyone was happy, so he named her Sweetbull.

Hector was 5 feet 8 inches tall, spoke fluent Spanish and all right English. He had had a hard life but was very street-wise. He could achieve a lot but loved fast, easy money. I guess who could blame him. How easy life would be to just hit the lottery, well, the big one.

Brand's thoughts were thinking about the job and how the money was a bit too easy. With that, his iPhone went off, and Hector was calling.

"Bro, Bubba said ok, but he was pissed." As Brand was still half lost in his thoughts, Hector waited for a reply. Both men sat in silence. It was ultimately Hector who broke it. "Bro, we're on, but we have to meet up... to set it up."

Brand just knew this was going to be trouble, and yet lately, the act of self-preservation had seemed to fade. He was now prone to sudden fits of rage. Actually, rage doesn't accurately define it. It came instantaneously, and even though he had control over it, he just didn't care and lately would let it play out regardless the consequences.

Hector's voice brought Brand back to reality. "Bro, you there? Stop messing around. Where do you want to meet them?"

Now Brand felt like answering, "There's a bar off 15th street called ROCKY. There's a table at the very back, off to the right. We can meet there."

Hector also seemed to be having anger issues hearing the tones in his voice. "Bro, WHO CARES where we sit!"

Brand could feel his annoyance rising, but he managed to contain it. "I have my reasons. You want me there or not? For that matter, why does Bubba want me to film a haunted house for him? There are plenty of people that will do it for far less?"

Hector, much more quietly, said, "Bro, you're getting a name on the street. People that deal with you, bad things happen if the deal goes bad. Bubba says he wants the baddest man he can find because this house ain't no joke. Him and Ben do that YouTube stuff and make big money. They will camera you up, and all you do is walk around."

Chapter 2

ROCKY

To say the bar ROCKY had seen better days was being nice. In truth, it was a dump. Dark in general with touches of past glamor. Like a fighter that's been beat but will not go down. Its wooden walls had pictures of people no one knew, with tables and floors having bruises from many past encounters.

Yet the owner, Joey, loved her like a biker loves his bike. Brand owned a Harley-Davidson Fat Boy, so he understood that type of love. Brand named his bike, "Matilda" which was chosen from a Tom Waits song "Four Sheets to the Wind in Copenhagen," or better known as "Waltzing Matilda."

Joey and Brand had common interests, including watches and the great past fighters that never seem to be replaceable. Brand had helped him once in the past during tough times. Joey had never forgotten. He was that kind of guy. That with the fact that the bar seemed never to be even half full.

The corner table recessed from the main wall of tables was always available for Brand.

Hector, Bubba, and Ben were already there, waiting and all were not happy. Bubba was a big southern man about 35. He was overweight, but he knew how to use that extra weight. His size was intimidating, and his presence very loud.

He seemed to take pleasure in making people uneasy and awkward moments were just fine to his liking. Ben was almost the complete opposite. He was lean, average build and very low mannered. Bubba was saying he doesn't like to wait. Hector was trying to pacify Bubba, saying he's the real thing.

Hector said, "Bro. What, you expect him to come early?"

When entering the bar, the tables were to the right and the bar adjacent to the left. Way back in the corner, there was a four-foot recess with an area big enough for a table of four. One person had to sit by the very back wall with no view of the bar or any tables or patrons.

Hector was on one side and Ben on the other with Bubba sitting across from the back wall.

Hector was on the left of Bubba and could see the complete bar and door without turning his head. He was relieved when Brand finally appeared.

Brand arrived with a small duffel bag. Hector was already starting to feel uneasy. He knew Brand was very punctual and never carried more than he needed. Brand seemed to grin when he saw the back wall seat open.

Brand studied human nature, and he wanted that seat in the back. Human nature usually likes seeing the exit. To feel safe knowing you are not stuck in the back with virtually no vision of the common area. And human nature won again as all were seated exactly where Brand desired.

Brand always had a plan and then a backup plan, just in case. Plan A was that Bubba would give Brand the $1,200.00, all upfront, and then three days from now they would all meet at the house. Or more precisely, at the driveway because Bubba and Ben didn't want to go near the home.

Plan A did not happen!

Brand had to shuffle around the others to get to the open seat. Working his way past Hector's back to the available chair. His duffle bag didn't make it any easier. Finally, he settled in and was looking intensely into Bubba's eyes. There was tension before a word was even spoken. Bubba was the first to speak.

"You don't look very tough. You know what I think? I think for six hours, you get 600."

Brand never took his eyes off Bubba. He never moved an inch. Just said in a cold voice, "Okay, just show me the 600. Put it on the table, and spread it out so I can see it."

Hector could tell what Brand was doing, he liked to take control even in accepting the lessor offer. He was trying to control the action.

What Hector didn't know was that while he never took his eyes off of Bubba and looked like he had never moved, he actually was moving his arm and hand. Like a news broadcaster, you have to speak without moving or it becomes annoying to the audience. By keeping eye contact with Bubba at all times, Bubba never saw a thing.

Bubba turned to Ben and said, "Give me 600," with a big smile. Once the money was in Bubba's hands, he laid it out on the table spreading it across as he had been instructed to do. There were two $100 bills, and the rest were in twenties. As that was happening, Brand had unlocked a large knife on the side of the duffel bag and with a swooping motion coming from behind his back, going above his head he landed the knife an inch from the side of Bubba's hand, pinning the money between the knife and table. It happened so fast everyone was stunned.

Now with a colder and deeper voice than before, Brand stated, "Now, I am going to take THAT 600, and unless you put another 600 on the table, I'm walking. I may have a gun in my other hand under the table pointed at your balls. So, what do you say, Bubba?"

All the while this is happening Brand's eyes had never left Bubba's face. At that moment, everyone looked at Brand, and sure enough, his other hand was under the table out of sight.

Bubba looked white and grunted, "Give him the other 600."

Then a grin came on Bubba's face, and he loudly said, "Damn, you're a real badass," and in a lower voice, "We good?"

Brand was always disappointed when he had to use violence. He liked to feel his powers of persuasion would always win the day. Violence was just the easy way out.

Ben had, at this point, put the other 600 on the table as Bubba's was now not taking his eyes off Brand.

Brand started pulling the knife out from the table and bills. Scooping the money, Brand let a big grin spread across his face. Perhaps he and Bubba had more in common than he initially had thought.

"Of course, we will meet in three days at the driveway, and six hours from then you'll have your video." It was a weird exchange. He had almost cut Bubba's hand, threatened that he may have a gun pointed at Bubba's balls with the coldest voice, and a second later was acting as nothing had happened. It was unsettling.

Once the money exchange was done, Brand was all happy and wanted to eat big. As for Hector and Ben, they seemed subdued. Bubba had gotten what he wanted, a real badass, and was now wondering if that was a good thing. He was used to dominating via his size and manner. Brand had gotten the better of him and he didn't like it, but for now, he was accepting it.

Chapter 3

GETTING READY

Darrell Green was a long-time friend of Brand, who he had met in his military days. Brand was never officially in the service but had performed work for the government that most would say was spy work. From Brand's perspective, Darrell was one of those people that just seemed to love you and are always there when needed. Many times, he would come to Brand's assistance which seemingly had no benefit to Darrell.

But things rarely are what they seem, and people's motives have complex agendas that sometimes take decades to accomplish.

After his call with Brand, which he said he would do some research and get back to him, he immediately called Lieutenant Colonel Bolt.

"Sir, Subject 9 contacted me regarding research on a haunted home. He is being paid to record ghosts. How would you like me to proceed?"

After a short moment of silence, Bolt responded to Darrell, "Do the research, then report back."

Darrell had been sub-working for the Lieutenant for years now and knew they were always monitoring Subject 9. But today, whether it was a moment of conscience or just strong curiosity, he pressed the issue.

"Sir, can we meet?" Bolt felt like there must be more to this issue than Darrell was conveying, so to make sure there were no mishaps, he decided to agree to the meeting.

He said, "Location B will be fine. Let's say 90 minutes."

Lieutenant Colonel Bolt never wanted to be surprised, so he felt good that all bases would be covered. On the other hand, Darrell, who had requested the meeting, was now not sure how it would go. The truth is, he was just curious about what "RBs" really are or, more accurately, what they really can do. Now he wished he had never asked to meet.

Roy had let Brand stay on his farm with no rent payments. Brand had strongly insisted on paying him something and had tried on numerous occasions to pay him something, but Roy and Sarah, with their three children, were a different type of people.

They immediately warmed up to Brand even though they barely knew him. Brand had never helped them in any way before. Roy was a huge man standing 4 inches above 6 feet with hands that were not only large but incredibly strong. All of those days working on the farm had calloused his hands terribly, but not his heart.

He worked hogs but also had many other types of animals on the farm. He even grew orange and banana trees, selling the fruits to the locals at great prices.

On top of his farm, Roy also took odd jobs. Building swimming pools and other jobs requiring either strength or nerves. In regards to his truck, it could pull anything ½ or ¾-ton or bigger with no problem. His words.

Basically, with Roy's help, Brand had been able to buy the 5th wheel, and Roy had towed it to his farm. They leveled the ground, and Roy had helped with all the hookups and connections. So, when Roy would ask for some little favor, Brand was all too happy to comply.

Roy approached him now. "Hate to bother you, but could you watch over the fruit stand? It will only be for three hours?"

Brand had so little contact with people at this point in his life that the few who came by were a welcome distraction. "Sure, no problem."

Oneco was off the main paths of Florida. You have Tampa at the top and Miami and Glades down South, with the center having Boca Raton on the East and Sarasota/Bradenton on the West. But if you go away from the ocean or gulf towards the center, you get to the other Florida.

People were different in the other parts of Florida. You might say really laid-back or nicer than need be. Some, of course, were crazier than society could handle, but others not having the negativity that large metropolitan centers can bring.

Amy was one of the nice ones. She was a young 33 and had a beauty that was natural. Her hair started brown and down her back, then shoulder length with green highlights. Later ear level and totally black. Between the Goth look and the girl next door, she could be or look however she wanted. She loved to wear many rings and chokers plus necklaces, giving her a 1969 look.

On a deeper level, she was shy but always spent time listening to others. And on a much deeper level, she had a lot to say, was amazing, and made Brand, a romantic by heart, dare to even think again that love could make a way.

Young people think of love being directly connected with sex. To an older person, just having someone showing interest in their life, especially from a young person, feels so nice. It is very flattering to an old ego for them to spend their time and seemingly to care. This was a form of love that Brand now desired.

Seconds later, his brain hit reality, telling him she was just one of the nice ones, grinning to himself with a chuckle. Too young, too pretty, she had a boyfriend, and a girlfriend, which he believed were at different times but had no knowledge of that. Nice people tended to throw Brand off.

Today Amy arrived at the fruit stand with her hair back to shoulder level with browns and lighter tones mingled thru-out. There were two other people there who seemed to be enjoying their time together more than for the quest of some cheap oranges.

Amy gave Brand a smile and asked how he was doing? The thing with Amy was she would look at you, ask a question, and really be listening. Not like ready to make another statement and can't wait for you to finish. No, she would listen to every word and comment directly to your statement.

He gave her a grin and said, "Well, for an old man, I am still able to get out of bed," his grin getting bigger. She responded by just giving him a look that was saying, really, how are you doing.

He responded again by saying fine, but there was a touch of loneliness that they both shared. And when they looked again in each other's eyes, they both felt a camaraderie that was unspoken. Brand asked her how she was doing which she looked down for a moment and then a smile with the answer fine.

He noticed she had a new tattoo which he thought was just an artistic design, but she explained that it was based on Japanese comic books.

The rest of the time at the fruit stand went uneventful, but Brand still had Amy on his mind. She never would acknowledge he was old, as he would mention it to her in conversation, but she would never respond to that subject. That was another reason he really liked her. When you're old, it is nice at times to just forget that fact. Being around certain young people made that much easier.

They had become text buddies talking about many different subjects. To Brand, it seemed lonely people seemed to find comfort with other lonely people.

Sweetbull was the best thing in Brand's life, period. He got her, or better said, saved her when answered a phone call from her owner. At that time, he was renting out a room, and the two girls had occupied it for time. They had brought two dogs. One was a puppy only five weeks old, little Sweetbull. After some unfortunate instances, he had had no choice but to evict the girls. He had missed having both dogs around dearly.

The girls had been lovers. One was blessed with beauty and brains, her body being very thin the other was even prettier but was still trying to find her purpose in the world. They would fight all the time and lived a life where one just dominated the other. It was hard to watch, and when the domination started on Brand, it was time for them to go.

About five months later, he received the call. "Hey, I know we haven't talked but do you want Sweetbull?"

The answer was, without hesitation said simply and firmly, "Yes." From that point on, they slept, ate, and played together except when Brand had jobs come in. Only people who own pets would understand.

Simply put, in the twilight of his time, Sweetbull was his life. He definitely didn't worry about his own safety. In the event that something ever happened to him, he had already made plans for Sweetbull.

It surprised him that people never liked to acknowledge old age. He knew at best he would have maybe ten more years. Given his family's history in addition to his lifestyle, not to mention his current state of mind, the end was within sight. Whether it was his children, which he had two, or his friends that were fifty and under, they never wanted to acknowledge that his time was short.

Even Amy, who was very real about things, would never address that issue. To him, that made no sense. It was like denying what is right before your eyes.

Brand had given up on finding happiness in the form of true love, except if it was with animals. He joked that if you wanted "Unconditional" love, go to the animal shelter and save a life.

Chapter 4

REALITY BENDERS

Lieutenant Colonel Bolt had been in charge of Subject 9 for over a decade. He had worked on the Reality Bender project or better known as the RBs project, for more than 26 years, and he still was apprehensive about it.

The idea that people could bend reality was crazy until you dove into the science. There it showed an entirely different picture. From the ball and peg test, to many others, they clearly showed that subjects could sway the outcome of experiments to a statistically significant degree.

In the ball and peg test, there is a board with pegs inserted from the top to the bottom. Then a ball is dropped from the top and works its way down to the bottom, hitting different pegs on their downward spiral. Typically, they will make a 49/50 distribution at the bottom, which is split into two buckets. Certain subjects could tip the average past that to a level that previously would have been thought of as impossible. They were changing the laws of physics to achieve an outcome they desired.

As they studied the phenomenon, it became clear that they were getting the weakest subjects. The strong candidates were doing things that were hard to imagine or believe.

For example, in the war of 1914, when there was a truce at Christmas time, both armies stopped fighting and became friends on the field of battle just for that one day. That has never happened before or after. That was a strong Reality Bender that could modify not just physics but human behavior. From there, they started to realize the true significance of those abilities.

So, procedures and protocols were put into place to study the strongest ones in a natural environment. Meaning, constant watch on what the subject is saying and doing to see if correlations to events can be determined.

In Subject 9's case, it was observed him having an argument with a neighbor a year ago about whether more people died in wars or by diseases. Subject 9 had stated diseases had killed more people than all of the wars combined. The neighbor, a military man, eventually left shaking his head like Subject 9 was crazy. Less than a month later, a virus started in China. Was it a connection? Who knows, but Bolt's job was to monitor and follow where the trail lead him. One of the main protocols was that everyone was on a need-to-know basis.

In regards to Subject 9, every area that he had lived in, crime had gone down and the neighborhoods had improved. In some areas, this effect was very wide. Every company he had left on bad terms with either closed or had a complete management change within 18 months. But while he was there, the company had been doing very well.

His effects were mostly subtle but observed over long periods of time, and after being collated over many different events, a pattern started to emerge. It was like watching a clock, you never see the hands move, and yet the effect is evident.

Bolt arrived at location B, a park not far from his office. The idea of really having a private meeting was foreign to most in the security business. If they really want to listen, they will find a way. Making it harder for them and always keeping a good sense of paranoia never hurt.

There was a bench that was isolated on the left side with running water from a stream nearby. Truth be told, he loved that spot and always felt a sense of peace there. As he checked the time, Darrell was making his way up the path.

Darrell started by saying, “Sir, I have done preliminary research on the house, and there is definitely a source of dark energy there. It could very well hold a fixed portal with variable time openings coming about every 18 years.” Bolt listened but was waiting for why they were really meeting. This information could have been provided by a secure line.

Darrell continued, “So, what do you want me to tell him?”

Bolt had good instincts, and he learned to live by them. He started, “Why are we having this meeting?” His voice showed he was getting aggravated, and Darrell knew he would have to come out with it.

Darrell now started again with, “Sir, off the record, why all the worry about RBs? From what I see, they hardly affect anything?”

Now Bolt was annoyed. Darrell knew better. For all Bolt knew, this could be a test on him from some other group. Did Darrell really expect him to discuss this just anywhere and to someone so low on the hierarchy?

Bolt looked at him for quite some time without saying a word, then he stated, “This meeting is terminated. Never ask or mention RBs again unless specifically needed. This will go against you, you understand.”

Darrell looked like a broken man, “Sorry, sir, what actions would you like done?”

Bolt was ready to address that. “Send me a complete report on secure channels. Provide a portable self-powered disrupter. It may help Subject 9.”

The only thing heard after that was, Yes, sir!

Chapter 5

HECTOR'S PROBLEM

Hector was in trouble with a gang over money; imagine that. For all of Hector's street-wise smarts, he wasn't a fighter. People who know that on the street will take advantage.

Brand spent most of his time at home with Sweetbull these days. To most, he was in good shape and could hold his own in most situations. But to himself, he felt old and thought more about his future death than present living. A warrior's death is all he asked for.

He wasn't too surprised when Hector stopped over. Brand was figuring that he wanted to go over the meeting with Bubba and Ben.

But Hector looked way too scared for that.

"Bro, you gotta help me, please, just talk to them. They may listen if it comes from you."

Brand was going to blow it off, but this time the desperation in Hector's voice was too much.

He looked at Hector and said, "Sure, I'll help. Let's go talk to them."

Hector hesitated, startled. He had imagined having to beg Brand to help him.

"Bro, you want to go right now?"

Brand was already putting his leather jacket on, and his only reply was, "Yes."

As Hector was driving, he explained that there was a gang that thought he owed them for a drug deal gone bad. Hector had made the initial connection for the buyer and sellers, the gang. The deal had gone badly, and the gang was robbed of the drugs and wanted Hector to pay for them since he had made the connection. Of course, that is not how it works, and it seemed like they were taking advantage of Hector, knowing he would not fight back.

When they arrived at the back lot of the convenience store, Brand was not impressed with their setup. It was a little gang. There were only three people hanging out against a wall. One was the leader, one the go-do boy, and the enforcer.

As Brand was surveying the situation, he made his mind up quickly on the actions he should take. They were really just punks and simple reasoning would not work. A good threat would also be useless as punks don't respect that type of thing.

There was a table with some paper and drug paraphernalia. Brand started to take his coat off and handed it to Hector. Then his two watches, three rings, and pendant, all the time never addressing the three men watching him. Hector was being very careful with all of Brand's stuff, but all could tell that Hector was really scared.

Brand picked up some loose sheets of school paper sitting on the table and started to roll them up to create a sharp point at one end, forming a cone. All while never addressing the three men who just stared. Then he looked over to the enforcer, who was called Tiny because he was huge. He had to be a foot taller than Brand and was made of pure muscle.

The kind of man that would allow you to give him your best punch, and it would do nothing. A man that would break your neck like a chicken wing and not have a second thought.

Brand, with his open hand, moved his fingers towards himself in a gesture saying, come on, Tiny, let's do it.

Tiny was not scared to fight anyone. His size and strength made him a formidable opponent regardless of who he fought.

Brand had always said your strongest weapon in any fight is your head, not strength, size, or endurance. Just using your brains. People who are bigger, stronger, and quicker usually are overconfident, which can be used to their demise.

What happened next happened so fast that if you had to look away for 20 seconds, you'd miss everything except the outcome.

As Tiny stood up from where he was sitting, Brand moved so quickly it was like he ran right into Tiny's chest. In fact, that was exactly what he had done, but he had his arms outstretched above his shoulders. Like if you were saying with your arms, I surrender. It startled everyone, especially Tiny, but Tiny regained his focus and started his move to end Brand.

When you're fighting a bigger opponent, you need to get in close so their arms won't be able to hit you. Then you have access to their personal space and hopefully can use it to win.

Tiny started to bend down to get his arms in the right spot to break Brand's back. In doing so, he lowered his head, forgetting that Brand still had two arms and ten fingers available.

Brand only had seconds to make his plan work. With his right hand, he stabbed the end of the pointed paper into Tiny's right eye with force. Eye injuries are one of the most painful injuries to receive. It will stop all your focus and demand immediate attention. Tiny was now feeling incredible pain and had loosened his grip. Brand dropped the paper and, with his big knuckles, drove a punch right into Tiny's throat. A very hard punch that broke Tiny's esophagus. At that point, the fight was over.

Tiny, who was having trouble breathing, went down. Once you can't breathe, you're going down no matter how big or strong you are. Brand was pushing away from Tiny as he was meeting the ground choking.

Brand looked at the boss who had not moved and yelled, "Call 911. Your friend needs help and a hospital." Hector, who thought they were both going to be shot, was as frozen as the boss and the go-do guy.

Then Brand looked at the boss and asked, "Are we done?" which was replied with a head shake up and down.

At that point, the boss yelled at the go-do guy to "Call 911 NOW!"

Then without any hurrying, Brand put back on his silver customized with two big Bs Turquoise ring, gold Cat's Eye ring, black Onyx ring, the Chinese pendant, the Pakistan brown leather jacket being the Han Solo style. His AVI-8 Gunmetal Grey Spitfire and Apple Watches.

Hector still looked frozen, so Brand said, "Give me the keys. I'll drive."

Once in the car and on the way home, Hector seemed to wake up.

"Bro, what were you thinkin'? You -- we going to get killed!"

Brand had seen this before. Some men had never seen real violence in front of them, never been close to a life and death situation.

"Relax, we're fine. Their enforcer was just destroyed by a 63-year-old man with a piece of paper. They're not coming for more."

Hector was still in shock, saying, "Bro, all I wanted was you to ask them nice." He said it slowly, like he was talking in his sleep. Not much more was said until Brand parked the car and Hector got out to get into the driver's seat.

Brand looked into his eyes, and Hector knew he could not look away.

"I have fixed your problem, but now you owe me," it was said matter of fact, but there was no mistaking the intention.

Hector shook his head slightly up and down and said quietly, "Yea, bro."

Then he seemed to come back to life and said, "Bro, I played to Bubba that you were real badass, but I didn't really believe. Now, after seeing you work Bubba and Tiny, bro, you really are da man!"

Brand now was serious, even looking troubled, and said, "Hector, I am no bad ass, and never believe the best and the worst said about you. That stuff can become your worst enemy."

Hector and Brand had two days left until the meetup with Bubba and Ben. Brand still had to get back to Darrell to see if he had any information on the house. You can never have too much information unless you're betting on football. But that's a different story. With all these thoughts, Amy still crept into his mind.

The next morning was a beautiful Florida day for March. Little brisk in the morning but wonderful by 10 a.m. Brand was out back with Sweetbull doing what they did a lot. Sweetbull was playing, digging, guarding, and killing things. She loved to kill the little lizards and had already finalized two snakes in her three years of life. Brand was just enjoying nature, which he found most enjoyable in his later years. People, only in small groups for short periods of time, but relaxing with nature and Sweetbull had become full-time love.

At around 9:45 a.m., his iPhone went off, and it was Darrell on the other end. He said he had information and a device that might help. Brand set up the meeting for 12:00 p.m. so they could have lunch together. That was one thing Brand disliked about being alone. He liked company when eating. Of course, he had Sweetbull, who he had to share half his meals with. The interchange of discussion during eating was not quite the same, though with Sweetbull.

Chapter 6

MEETING WITH DARRELL

Darrell Green was an oddity to Brand. He appeared to know everyone that Brand seemed to need now and then. Always ready and willing to help, never being critical or positive of his actions, just interested and helpful.

Like today all he had asked was if he could do some research on a haunted home he was going to stay at. Darrell was one for facts, so Brand explained all that he knew, the date, the times into and out of the home, and what he was supposed to do. Brand understood that to help someone, it is best to have all the pertinent facts.

They met at Marina Jack in Sarasota, an eatery off the water with a pleasant view of the sailboats and powered crafts. Of course, the fish didn't actually come from there, but the illusion worked.

Darrell was 49 with a slim muscular build. Short light brown hair and spoke a lot like Tucker Carlson.

Today he was all business, "Hello Brand, I have researched that house and lots of bad things have happened there. First..." but before he could continue, Brand interrupted.

"Brother, did you write it all down?"

Darrell replied, "Yes, but..."

Again Brand interrupted, "Then I will read it all. What I want to know about is you mentioned a device." Brand loved high-end electronics. He knew there were some really fantastic hidden technologies that could change the world.

Brand loved history, and certain individuals like Nikola Tesla were a history unto themselves. We still don't even use his best creations and have never changed his AC electricity since it was developed. So, if Darrell had a device that might help him in a haunted house, that was what he really wanted to hear about.

Darrell seemed a bit taken aback. He really wanted to tell him about the house, but his notes were always very detailed, so it seemed like he said to himself I tried and then went into talking about the device.

He began by, "This device works like a sound blocker except in its case it blocks energy frequencies. First, it has to detect the frequency being projected and then find the exact opposite frequency amplifying it to cancel the projected frequency. It's called a disrupter. Being that there is no power in the home, it works off batteries, so all you have to do is activate it, and it does the rest. Any questions?"

Now Brand had many questions, "How long till it registers the frequency and how long till it's nullified?"

Without waiting for those answers, "How long will it last? Does it have a power bar?"

But the questions kept coming, "Has it been tested in the field?"

Darrell knowing how Brand was, just started answering the questions in the order given.

"It is undetermined how long; it depends on the frequency. Once it does lock on the incoming signal, it can disarm it quickly. But how long it will last depends on the power of the incoming signal. No, it does not have a power bar, and it has been tested in the field, but each situation is different. This has very limited power. Of course, if we had a stable power source, the bigger units are much more reliable."

Brand was impressed, figuring it couldn't hurt, and thanked Darrell but had one last question, "Where do you get this stuff? I am not putting you at risk, right?"

Darrell looked at him for a good minute and said, "We've been friends for over seven years. I care about you. Make sure you read the report, and no, I just have connections."

The actual disrupter was quite large. They went to the parking lot, and Darrell had a truck with the disrupter laying on its side. It had wheels on the bottom and was about 4 feet tall and 2½ feet wide and deep. It looked like a speaker box from a concert you see on stage.

"Somehow, I thought it would be smaller," Brand said, "You will have to drop it off at my place, okay?" Darrell didn't mind at all. At least, that is what he conveyed.

Lieutenant Colonel Bolt always had a personal diary. It was an old habit that his father had said would come in handy more times than not. Once you get used to doing it, the habit lasts for life. So, as had been done every day in the past, the paper black book diary, which in today's world is the most secure form of secrets, was taken out, and entries were added.

As he wrote about the day, it occurred to him that he had created at least half the procedures and protocols for the RBs. One protocol was to never let the RB know of himself personally. Just knowing who you are, they may affect you with no way to determine you have been affected. Now he was going to see how an RB does against a demon.

It would be an interesting event. Of course, it's never fair. Whoever is the stronger will always win. That is why he gave him the hope of a disrupter. Who knows, maybe he helped our side while staying in protocol. But he also really wanted to see if the effects Subject 9 produces could be more direct. Maybe the encounter would break his shell or take him to the next level.

In regards to demons, they are just entities from other dimensions with bad intentions. We call them demons, but in reality, they are just another life form with certain advantages that we don't possess.

The worry about what happens if we lose Subject 9 is always a concern. Sometimes in history, you can see where the death or birth of one person changes the world as we know it. Sometimes the world changes very quickly for no apparent reason. These changes may be related to powerful RBs that we are unaware of.

His retirement is coming, and then he will be just on the advisory board. Not having to handle the responsibilities of critical decisions that could possibly affect the world.

When Brand was back home, he contacted Hector, letting him know he had equipment that needed to be transported to the haunted home. It was valuable, so it needed to be handled gently.

Hector replied, "Bro, my cousin got a truck. I'll bring it and pick you and the stuff to the job." That is the thing about Hector. It was the reason. Brand liked him. If he said he would do it, he does it. Brand hated liars, and Hector had never broken that trust.

Another beautiful day in Florida. Brand still had not looked at the report created by Darrell. The event was tomorrow, but now he had a disrupter. A big grin appeared. What possibly could go wrong? He had that gut feeling that everything from this point on was going to all go his way.

He had slept well and felt great. At his age, you never knew which part of the body will decide to strike next with pain. After brushing his teeth, shaved and showered, plus a little glow for his hair. Now some clothes that make a man feel that special way. In Brand's case, that would be something that comes from afar and looks really expensive.

His watches, rings, and pendant with some wrist jewelry, yes he was feeling great, so when he heard the knock on his door, he was greeted with a welcomed surprise.

There was Amy. They had started texting back and forth pretty regularly and had really started to get to know each other. She had said that sometime soon, she was going to stop over and surprise him. Well, today was that lucky day.

"Hello, miss Amy, welcome to my humble abode," Brand said with a big smile. She started up the four steps on the stair arriving in the living room. The kitchen was left of the living room, and the bedroom was to the right of the stairs.

She looked great, but that was usual. What was new was that they were together alone in his place. That was a first, and the amazing thing was it felt so natural to Brand. There was no awkwardness. In fact, they were communicating much better than by text. It was wonderful; the day could get no better. And if it could get no better, then it could only get worse.

She spent over two hours with Brand giving promises of more visits to come. At one point, she even showed him her belly button ring, and he begged her not to pierce anything else. They had a great time, but like all great times, they must end. Before she left, she came in close and gave Brand a long tight hug. It seemed to last forever and only a second.

After Amy's visit, Brand finally decided to look into the research Darrell had provided, and he had promised to read. It wasn't that big, but it was dark.

It started with the land. In the year of 1701, the tribe known as the Terawak had used that area as a burial ground, but not for their chiefs and warriors. It was reserved for the worst of their kind.

The land was avoided for over 100 years. During that time, it was surmised that the reason the worst were buried there was that a great evil came every generation. This evil makes men and women crazy. Seeking to kill others or themselves. Even the animals avoided that area. That lasted for many generations, but in the summer of 1809, it was taken over by the United States government, and a settlement was created.

But just as the Indians had said, people who lived on that land went crazy. The records get unclear about when but around the late 1800s or early 1900s, the home that resides there today was built.

From there, the records showed over six families had moved in, only to find calamity. Some of the stories were so horrific that Brand didn't read them fully. Just skimmed over them. All in all, it was everything that great horror movies are made of. Well, slasher movies anyway. With the thought of going there tomorrow, his day was going from worse to downright awful.

Each family talked about evil being in the house. For some, it just brought terrible misfortune, but for others, it made them pay the ultimate price, the lives, and sanity of the occupants.

Darrell had notes attached, which stated the worst occurrences happened approximately every 18 years. Looking at the last really bad occurrence, Brand estimated it had occurred about 19 years ago. Looks like the evil was a bit overdue.

Then in his mind, he remembered Hector saying it had to be on the 27th. Now he was wondering why that day. What did Bubba and Ben know that made them so scared they wouldn't even go near the house? Why were they emphatic that the job needed to be done on the 27th? Brand was getting spooked. There was no way to deny the danger, yet he knew he would have to see it through.

Another note stated to bring salt, make a circle, and stay in the circle. A side note said to bring the disrupter into the circle too. It stated to wait until the dark source is strongest as the disrupter will do the most damage at that time.

Obviously, Darrell had gotten scared too. That's why he had gotten the disrupter and had wanted Brand to read all the notes. The truth was that before the notes, Brand was feeling good and had thought this job would be easy. Now, he wanted to bring more flashlights, candles, extra salt, and whatever else he could think of to protect himself from whatever evil lived in that home.

At this time of year, the sunlight goes out by about 7:00 p.m., and he was to enter the home an hour before that. Now he was thankful for cutting the time to six hours instead of twelve, but six hours is a long time in a home that has had that much blood shed.

In all the reports, many of the occupants had guns, but that only helped them to kill themselves or others. It had never seemed to stop the evil that permeated there.

The thoughts of just backing out, giving back the money, and enjoying life with Sweetbull were flooding his brain. He knew deep down, though, that he would have to go through with it. He had to. In for a penny, in for a pound. This was one of his favorite old English expressions that meant once you have made a commitment, you must see it through. There were a lot of negative things that you could say about Brand, but he was loyal and true to his word. If he said he would do it, then he would make sure it was done.

Now, after Amy's visit and the Hector fiasco, he became reflective. It was not a pretty picture. Brand started to feel bad about Tiny. He knew Tiny would never be the same. That's the real problem with violence. Not the worry that he would get hurt. That had happened plenty of times. The real problem with violence is the effect and lasting impact on others. The feeling of blood on your hands. He had been reckless and looking to die. He knew that subconsciously.

He did like to balance things, always thinking about the double edge sword.

Too orderly is bad. Too spontaneous is bad. You have to always balance the two. It is like that with all things, he believed.

He was angry at himself about Tiny. Trying to justify that if Tiny were smaller, he could have done less damage.

With these thoughts in Brand's mind, Amy was far away. He was now completely focused on the house. He had only read two stories fully, and that was enough. The people who lived there had done horrible things. Slowly cutting body parts from a loved one but cauterizing the wound so they could cut as much as possible while the person lived as long as possible. Then cooked and ate those parts while teasing the victim about how good they tasted and what part would be cut off next.

Brand had been in life and death events before. Sometimes it is you or them. In those times, what is done is not out of anger. It is an instinct of survival. Either way, you don't feel bad at the time, you're alive. Regret does not come until later.

This was different, though. Slow torture for the love of torture and to be done to a loved one for as long as possible. He was having real reservations about doing the job tomorrow.

He would get up early and buy more supplies. More flashlights, plenty of salt and crosses, he thought with a grin.

Then again, Social Security only goes so far. He always had enough but never too much more than that. Doing odd jobs to get extra money bought all the special things in life he wanted. Like his watches, jewelry, or clothes collections, but there was never a rainy-day fund.

Sweetbull was always the first to go to bed and the last to get up. That night Sweetbull was having bad dreams, as Brand could tell by her growling. Unfortunately for him, he could not sleep at all.

Being tired while doing anything is bad. Being scared and tired was worse. Now time would not stop. Each time he checked, the clock moved an hour. Noon was approaching, with Sweetbull only being twice out but wanting more.

She always wanted more, more time together, more love, but always more food. Looking at her gave Brand some peace. In his mind, he was thinking, those stories just spooked me. I'll be there on my own. I won't be able to hurt anyone else, and I am not hurting myself. I have a disrupter! I'll be fine.

Whether he would or would not did not matter. He had to do it, no matter how much right now, he wanted to call in sick. With that, he smiled to himself, thinking maybe it will be a glorious end. I could save someone before my death and kill the demon too. With that thought, he was ready and hungry.

Lieutenant Colonel Bolt was deep in thought. He felt like a puppet master. Like when he was young, and they had a toy called "Mouse Trap." You align all the pieces, and when one goes off, the next one follows until the end result nets you a mouse.

He knew more about Subject 9 than Subject 9 knew about himself. His agents Roy and Darrell were in close contact. Even Hector didn't know he was being played. Subject 9 was monitored by people and electronics 24/7. Right now, the only variable, besides the contest, between Subject 9 and the demon was Amy. He would have to take care of that. It was a loose end, a wildcard that could change everything.

He had found that keeping a constant equilibrium in regards to the subject's state of mind and body helps in maintaining the current state of affairs. Even if that state is not good, the possible outcomes could be much worse. Amy would have to go.

Chapter 7

THE HOUSE

After taking Sweetbull out for a walk and play, which mostly consisted of fighting over a stick or anything the other had. Brand got on Matilda and headed for some extra supplies.

Usually, his nerves were on edge when something big was going down. Once the event started, he would settle down and be fine. Today, however, his nerves were on fire. This house had him scared, and he had not even seen it. Now he understood why Bubba and Ben did not want to get too close. Neither did he.

Once home, he had another shower. He started to pack. He was just taking whatever he deemed essential. He decided not to bring guns or knives as he wanted no "accidents." No question the house had got to him. Checking the clock, it was 4:05 p.m. Hector was supposed to pick him up and take him there to the driveway by 5:30 p.m. for Ben to attach the cameras. After all, was said and done, Hector would take him home at midnight. He didn't plan on spending an extra minute there.

Hector arrived and seemed reserved, which was not his usual self.

"Bro, got the truck. She's a beauty." If Hector was reserved, Brand was already in semi-shock. Hector could tell things weren't good, and now he was feeling guilty dropping his buddy at a spot where no one else would go.

He started again, "Yo bro, we're ready to go. You good?" The answer was self-evident, so no reply came. Brand was all inside his head. He not only looked scared, he was scared. The stories were horrible. Now he wished he hadn't researched it at all. He would have been in better shape to deal with what was coming.

Brand tried to calm himself down mentally. He kept thinking maybe nothing will come. As Hector said, this is easy money. He kept repeating in his mind, *calm down, you got a disrupter*, hoping it would reassure him of his safety. It was an internal battle with many wins and losses.

Hector was right. The truck was a beauty. A low rider with a great paint job and special details that made you know the owner really loved her. Brand was surprised Hector's cousin lent him the truck, but certain families truly share.

Moments like this made Brand sad his children were so far away. Not being able to just drive and see them was hard. FaceTime was it. As his thoughts plunged, he really only wanted one wife to last to his ending days. Technically he had two but really three. In honesty, there were so many other women that not just the names were lost but the count too. He missed his family, having now only Sweetbull, who helped him survive.

They loaded the disrupter onto the truck. Brand had inspected it at home and had noticed some knobs so it could be adjusted manually. It had two switches, one that was set to the up position, which Brand assumed was for the automatic setting. He imagined if you push the switch down to the bottom position, the dials would come into play. The other switch was clearly marked as the on/off switch. Knowing Darrell, he had set it up to where it would be the most effective, and all Brand needed to do was hit the on switch at the right time for maximum effect.

Now time was moving quickly again, and the disrupter was loaded and strapped securely in place with blankets wrapped around it to help absorb any road bumps. Hector was driving, and there was little to no conversation on the ride there, except for Brand telling Hector to be there at the front door for his pickup at midnight and not a minute later.

Hector's answer, "Yea, bro. Got it."

In regards to where Hector drove, that information will be kept unsaid. That place still has much evil that pervades it, and the thought that others may go there must not happen.

The ride was lonely in many ways. There was no conversation within the truck but outside the landscape was baron. It was bare of any trees or any life for that matter. A place outside of time and people. Void almost of color. Looking like one pale shade that slowly changed as the light lowered.

Whatever Hector was feeling, he wasn't saying. Brand was starting to get back to himself, putting on his game face. Just before a battle, you have to get into a mindset of them or me. You know you're going to do things you never would except for in that moment. Whatever it takes, with no hesitation, no overthinking, just get it done.

After about 20 minutes of going down an unidentified road, they reached a gate that was about 4 feet in from the road. The gate itself was open, and there was nothing before or after it. Nothing across from it either. There was just an 8-foot by 4-foot space off a dusty dirt road.

Bubba and Ben were there with their truck parked half on and half off the road. Looked like they were ready to leave as fast as possible. Ben was all business.

Ben started in right away, "Wear this vest. I have cameras on the front and back. None of them will take your face unless you go by mirrors. Don't touch them unless I say so, understand?"

Brand looked at him and asked, "So, you're coming along?"

Ben was fast to say, "Oh NO! I have a short wave comm system. It's attached to the vest. You squeeze this button to talk to us."

Bubba was unusually quiet, but it seemed like admiration was in his eyes. He appreciated toughness. Here was a man doing something he was scared to do. For all of Bubba's loudness, he was no fool. He had enough information on the place to not want to be there.

Now time was moving so quickly minutes became seconds. Brand loved to smoke but had, for the most part, quit. Now there were about ten minutes before Hector would drive him to the house. It was back about 50 yards and to the left. He was going to go there early and set up the disrupter and salt circle but now decided not to spend an extra minute in that place. He pulled out a smoke, which he kept for times like this when he thought he might never have another. That cigarette was one of the best he ever had.

The house looked like an old farmhouse. Bigger than expected and not in too bad of shape. It was still standing, but as the truck got closer, it was apparent that the ground and home were cursed. There was a gloom that hung on it. A warning to all not to enter or enter at your own risk. Now there were less than 60 minutes before the sky became draped in total darkness.

The home had a porch that wrapped around it, with three steps rising to the porch's floor. About 6 feet further back, the double doors in front led inside. Hector, who was quiet and all business now, had unstrapped the disrupter and was wheeling it to the steps leading to the porch. Brand had a big duffel bag loaded with flashlights, salt, crosses, bibles, duct tape, water, food, and rope. The last item because it just felt right. Together they lifted the "portable" disrupter up the stairs letting it stand in front of the front door.

At that moment, Brand thought maybe the door is locked, but Hector, seemingly getting his thought, said, "Bro, it's open." There was an inch available to see through the front doors that guarded the home.

As Brand stood in front of the door, he thought about something he had that most others did not. Faith. Not the word but the real McCoy. A true 100% solid leap of faith, faith. When he had motioned Tiny to come and fight, there was not a doubt in his mind that he would survive. His trust in that faith was very different than most.

He remembered a joke, but that really wasn't, which made him grin before deciding to enter. The joke was there was a town that desperately needed rain. All of the people got together to pray for rain, but only one person brought an umbrella. He was that person.

He looked at Hector, who was going through an internal conflict, when he said, "I wait here for you, boss, you want?"

It was the first time Hector ever referred to him as boss, when Brand said, "No, you're good. Wait with Bubba and Ben. Midnight, not a second later!" Without hearing Hector, he knew he would be on time. Now, it was time to enter the house.

The house was already semi-dark regardless of the windows being without curtains and the little light left outside. The foyer was big and led to the kitchen. Off of the foyer on either side were rooms that were big, each with their own fireplace. The wood floors creaked underneath but were solid even after all these years.

It seemed the air itself had died inside this place, like something frozen in time where time itself has no power.

There were furnishings and so many things from so many owners. You could just tell that each who left, left everything, not wanting to take anything that may have been infected here with them. His mind was racing, but before any more exploration, he wanted to set up his safe zone.

He went to the left room off the foyer for reasons he could not say. Just a feeling it was safer, but in reality, it was the room the portal was in.

It was mostly empty but had junk around most of the walls. There was a couch, but it had long decayed into something else. It was pushed against a wall loaded with other things. Brand did not have to move much to create what he thought was a big enough circle defined by salt. A lot of salt! Then he placed candles inside and outside of the circle. He really didn't know much about it, so he just improvised in trying to be safe.

Next he placed flashlights within the circle and three situated on himself. He set a cross outside the circle, inside the circle, and worn one. No use yet for the duct tape or rope, but they were there just in case.

He had the disrupter already in the spot it needed to be in before he created the circle. His thinking was that he didn't want the wheels to displace the salt. Now that everything was ready, he looked again at the disrupter.

For the first time, he realized it did not even have a light. The on/off was labeled, but nothing more than that. If he did need this device, he was putting a lot of faith in something that displayed no love back.

Lieutenant Colonel Bolt seemed to never be relaxed. He thought of all the events that had happened while civilians and most of the military knew nothing about them. Most just wake, go about their business, and back to sleep. Thinking the world is just what they see on TV minus the monsters.

If they only knew how many monsters there were and how very close they really are to us. We are fighting an enemy that has been around from the beginning of our time. We are less than ants to them. Who would bow to an ant? And yet we still persist, and more important than that, keep gaining, inch by inch.

Bolt was deep in thoughts and was pleased he took some extra precautions with Subject 9 for the event this evening. From reports gathered regarding Subject 9, he seemed to be becoming more reckless concerning his personal safety.

As Hector drove back he felt bad about leaving his bro behind. He was still at war with himself, thinking nothing will happen to him. He's making the real money. He should take the big risks. Then the thoughts of, he just put his life up for you, he's like family, and you're being lame started to fill his head. Poor Hector was in quite an irritable state when he met back up with Bubba and Ben.

Bubba started, "So he went in, right!?"

Hector swung around, looking like he wanted to fight Bubba, saying, "Yeah, bro. You want to go check!"

Just then, Ben broke the tension by saying that they needed more light. The camera's video was poor. Everything was too dark.

Ben said on the radio to Brand, "Can you adjust the lights to full beam, or add more flashlights and candles? The picture is very dark."

At that, Brand, who was feeling a lot like Hector, responded, "You're welcome to come here and help!" With that, everyone became quiet and started to watch the monitors closely.

Ben did know his stuff and had three monitors going. A feed for the front monitor and back monitors plus a very wide-angle lens on the front going to the last monitor. Even with all of that and the lights, the monitor views were all hard to see. This was starting to anger Bubba, who was really bankrolling the operation.

Bubba said to Ben, "Dude, the picture sucks. Who's going to pay for this crap?"

Ben replied, "They don't pay, they view the website, and we make money. Just makes it look scarier. We're going to make good money from this. Trust me!"

It was totally dark now outside. The area that they were in had no streetlights or any lights except the moon to illuminate the lower surroundings. Because of this and the fact that it was a new moon, the darkness displaying the night's sky was amazing.

Brand was now in his safe spot. The circle of salt with the disrupter in front of him and the foyer to his right. Given the size of the house, he had barely surveyed it. Given the stories he had read about the home, he felt that he had surveyed enough. Looking at his watch, it was 6:15 p.m. He only had 5 hours and 45 minutes to go.

So far, nothing unusual had happened. Brand's senses were on extreme alert for any and all things. Thus, he would hear and see or smell things that ordinarily would pass the senses with no notice. So far, though, any real poltergeist or demon activity was absent.

He started to smile, thinking all of this fuss over nothing. He suddenly remembered the report Darrell had given him. He needed to keep sharp. Things are rarely what they seem.

Somewhere around 7:00 p.m., the atmosphere started to change. At first, it was like a vibration that made a subtle sound, but really it was more like an electric burst that was very weak. The air had a different charge to it. To Brand, this change in the environment was easy to detect.

The strangest thing was now that things were picking up, Brand's fear had dissipated. He had faced the end several times. Lucky for him, it did not happen. Now, finally, when it appeared that the battle was about to begin, all of his tension and stress was replaced with the adrenaline for the kill.

It came from the far-left corner of the room. At first glance, it seemed like heavy black dust, but it ruffled together, and a form started to materialize. Most of the body was fluxing, but the face stayed consistent.

It started to speak, "Oh, something different, how delightful." The tone of the voice was sarcastic but not overly menacing.

Then, “You’re different. You think you will be safe,” which was said diabolically.

“I will kill you and stretch time, so you will suffer for thousands of years!” Now the demon was fully coming out.

A normal person would have turned the disrupter on. For some crazy reason, Brand still was not scared. Nothing had really happened, but more importantly, the electricity in the air hadn’t changed.

Something in his gut said that when this demon would strike, he would feel the change prior to the event. There would be an increase in the static energy that was now present.

Brand had been in several imminent death situations, and after each one, on the next, he was calmer than the last. Fighting a demon to the death is an honorable end. So far, it was only threats. Just then, he wondered if the cameras were getting this. If yes, Bubba was getting his money’s worth.

Then everything changed. The static electric energy increased so much that his whole body was feeling an electric charge. As he was now ready to hit the switch, his body went haywire. It started in his gut with the feeling that his insides were being carved out. His intestines, large and small, felt like they were being cut into tiny pieces. He couldn’t even think, but things were going to get worse.

Now the demon was in delight, saying, “How’s that salt working out?” With laughter that contained more evil than anything Brand had ever heard.

Now the pain was a burning fire within his lungs, making breathing almost impossible. Then his private parts went to a burning cutting pain. The demon was having absolute pleasure in implementing the pain Brand was suffering. It brought this creator a high that cannot be imagined.

The demon’s face had brightened up. It looked like wet blood splattering its face from side to side. The evil in its eyes showing its utter delight in all that was happening. The electricity inside the room was lighting up like giant fireflies. There were bursts of reds and white with black blinking out the white. These blasts were so bright they hurt Brand's eyes.

At one point, Brand felt like he was going to lose consciousness, but that's when things changed. It was right before you feel the loss of everything around you. In that place, the pain disappears, and his mind was finally starting to think clearly. He still had not turned the disrupter on, which was first on his to-do list.

Even more important than that was his mind went to an old TV show called "Kung Fu." In one of the episodes, the main character was cursed by a sorcerer and had to focus his mind on tranquility to blank out the sorcerer's spell to win.

Brand, who was sitting in front of the disrupter, stood up. As he was getting up, he flipped the on switch. There was a little pain but nothing like before he had almost passed out. In his mind, there was only one thought. You cannot hurt me. I am in a peaceful place! His eyes were closed. He just kept thinking that one thought over and over again.

Hector, Bubba, and Ben were watching the monitors, but when the house started to light up, it became harder and harder to make out the picture clearly. When viewing the monitors during the bright flashes, you could see nothing.

But from dark to bright and vice versa, there was something in between daring to be seen.

Chapter 8

THE RESCUE

Hector could take no more. Without a word, he jumped into his truck and gunned it to the farmhouse.

As he went running in, this is what he saw. The demon had a reddish-black aura, while Brand had a blue light that seemed to surround him. The demon reddish-black pushing and crushing the blue aura Brand was generating. It would only be moments before the blue would be overtaken by the reddish-black. Both were in a hypnotic focus tuning everything else out.

Hector, who did have a gun, pulled the gun out and shouted something in Spanish that did not sound nice. Then shot six rounds into the demon's body.

The demon now noticed Hector. With one sweep of its hand, Hector was flown to the back wall. Hanging right in the center like you would pin a fly. He was in pain, that was obvious, but the fear on his face was terrifying to see. Hector's eyes were pleading for help. His face contorting trying to make words, but none would come.

During all this happening, it was really hard to judge time. Brand had come out of his trance state when Hector started shooting. It had brought him back, and he realized that he was no longer in any pain.

Now the demon turned his attention once again to Brand and said, "What a treat. Are there any more coming for you?"

This was said with such a cold, sadistic delight.

"I will kill them all but slowly, very slowly. They will curse your name and forget their own when I get done with them."

Brand could see Hector was in such fear. It made him angry, and in Brand's case, angry is not good for anyone. Once he became angry, it seemed to give him an internal power in addition to protection from pain.

It seemed the disrupter had not done a thing to help in fighting the dark entity.

The demon was regrouping, collecting strength from whatever source supplied it to him, and was getting ready for another attack.

Bubba was not happy. Not at all. He actually was really pissed about everything. The video was junk, and nobody would even want to watch it.

Worse than that, Bubba was not one to leave people behind. Brand went in for money. Hector had gone in for Brand. Both showed they had courage.

Bubba liked Brand. He was a badass which deep down Bubba wanted to be.

So with those thoughts in Bubba's mind, he jumped into his truck, yelled at Ben, who was at the monitors, "I'll be back," and then shouting at the windshield, "Damn Demon, you're not taking my boys!" He was speeding straight for the front door.

The battle had stopped for a brief few seconds. Hector was pinned to the wall, and Brand was showing signs of battle fatigue.

The demon had begun again and was saying, "Now I will burn your eyes out so darkness will be all you ever see," with a laughing giggle of someone so happy with themselves.

At that moment, everything changed again. The front door came crashing in with Bubba's truck behind it. Hector, Brand, and the demon all turned to see this. For a moment, everything stopped. Hector started to slide down the wall. Brand felt like he was in the eye of the hurricane, as everything around him had no effect upon his space occupied.

Now the demon was angry.

With what looked like two hands from the demon pushing out and towards Bubba's truck, the truck left the house with a bit less force than it had coming in, but still a lot, as it was pushed out.

The demon was raging, and that reddish-black aura was everywhere. It seemed to be making it hard to breathe. As the last air was being used, Brand was satisfied with this death. It could have been better but also far worse.

Bubba, to his credit, came back in again. This time shooting his gun seemingly everywhere. Sadly it was like running into a burning house with a glass of water. We were all doomed.

Just then, as the last of Brand's consciousness was going, he saw a bright light, brighter than any light he had ever seen. Seconds later, he felt himself slip out of this world.

Bolt had set up a safety plan consisting of two choppers with big disrupters that were sure to work. In actuality, only one was needed, but he liked to be prepared for all issues. He also had two dark units for extraction. Six men to get Subject 9 out and six to cover them. Included was also the "white sleep light," or what's usually called the "whitey" ready for use before the extractions and resolutions with any dark entity.

He had surveillance monitoring the area with night vision. The view was clear enough to see into the house, and they were ready to move on orders.

Once the truck hit the home, it was determined at that point to start extracting. This was fortuitous as Subject 9 was in really bad shape. They had the choppers plus ground support all using the whitey at the same time. It was so strong it even affected Ben, who was pretty far away.

The truth is for the disrupter to work efficiently, it has to be so strong that the human body can't survive its effects. The brain works on a relatively weak electrical charge, and being too close to the disrupter is bad. Giving Subject 9 a fake one to see if he could make it actually work failed. But it was worth the test.

Chapter 9

THE AFTERMATH

Brand had awoken in his bed feeling like he had been in a blender, and the blender had won. There were just too many parts to mention that hurt. His lungs hurt breathing. His eyes were too sensitive to light. His legs and arms were aching. The list just kept going on. Of course, all that didn't matter. What was important was Hector and Bubba.

Sweetbull was already outside, and with much grunting, pain, and willpower, he made it outside, down the stairs, and to Roy's home.

Before he got to the door, Roy was there saying, "Hey, big guy, you need to rest. Let me help you back to your rig."

Brand looked him in his eyes and said, "What happened to Hector and Bubba? How did I get here?" Roy could see there would be no use trying to do anything until answers were given.

Roy replied, "I overheard you, boys, talking about going there, and I just got a feeling you might need me. By the time I got there, the house had a truck half in and out of her, and thinking she may come down, I rushed in and got you and Hector out."

He stopped there, but by the look on Brand's face, he continued, "Then I called an ambulance for Hector and his friends, but knowing you hate hospitals decided to take you home, and we would fix you up. You just need rest, and you'll be back to new."

Brand had said nothing but then, "Roy, take me to the hospital. Now. Please."

By the time they arrived, Bubba had already been discharged. Hector was pretty much in the same shape as Brand. Beaten up bad but no major problems. In short, they were very lucky. He was also being discharged that day.

Lieutenant Colonel Bolt was again making entries into his diary. He now realized he had made a fundamental mistake with the RBs program. After listening to the analysis from his team, it appears Subject 9 did not totally fail. He was not able to generate the disrupter effects but was able to create a personal shield, that being the blue aura opposing the dark force's energy. It was not known he could do that. More tests were needed to further understand the depths of what these individuals could achieve.

The protocol of equilibrium will need to be modified. Being able to use sleeping gas in Subject 9's home and have our doctors check him out has been very effective. Roy was turning out to be quite an asset.

Hector was enjoying the beautiful Floridian day, which living there means it has to be just about perfect. He and Brand were on new lawn chairs. Well, really lounges with their own footrests. It was the best $24.97 spent. Brand had shared half the $1,200.00 with Hector. No, not $600 but $540.00 because Bubba had already given him $120.00 this making it exactly the same payout for both men.

Hector coming to his rescue trying to save him really touched Brand. Even Bubba was a hero to Brand. Both were brave under duress, and that says a lot about a man.

Hector started, "Bro, you got to check this thing out on YouTube. There's money we can make!"

He continued, "There this guy Jonas who wants us to..."

Right at that moment from the distance but coming straight to them was Amy. She was carrying a bag and looked like she was glowing.

Hector said, "Bro, I'll tell you later. I gotta go. Thanks for the extra money!"

Amy approached, and you could see she was so happy. Brand already was getting his spider-sense this would not end well for him.

She started, "I have some great and bad news," and as she said bad news, her head sank so slightly.

Brand said, "Well, what's the great news?"

She continued, "Well, my old girlfriend broke up with her boyfriend and asked me if I wanted to be her girlfriend. We were before but hid it. Now we are a couple out in the public!"

She was so happy, people who are in love are like that. The world just seems to be nicer, more beautiful to see and hear. Brand's heart felt crushed, but he was an actor, and with an Oscar performance, he lit up like he actually had found his own love and wished her the very best.

Inside he was dying as a coward dies a thousand deaths. He knew it was just his unrealistic hopes failing as he knew they would.

Almost as an afterthought, he asked, "So what's the bad news?"

She now dimmed a bit and communicated that her parents, who she lived with, got a great new job, but it is far away from here. Her girlfriend was going with her, so everything that mattered was fine.

She continued, "So this is goodbye. We can still text and video chat." She was so happy. For people you care about, that is all that you can ask for. He knew it would never have worked, but it still hurt.

Then she said, "Well, I have to go, but I got you just a little something," and placed the bag next to his lounge chair.

Brand got up quickly, knowing this would be his last hug. Amy came in close and started too hard in her squeeze, and Brand flinched, she lightened her grip, and he doubled his squeeze on her. He never wanted it to end, but all things end.

After she left, the air seemed to be empty. It was like a great hole that had just got bigger with no bottom in sight.

Then he looked down at the bag and the wooden framed box that was inside it. He pulled it out, and it said, "And Remember That Bad Times Are Just Times That Are Bad."

Part 2

Chapter 10

THE VIDEO

Brand Wright looked at his Sweetbull with unconditional love. The only other time he had known that was with his grandmother. He missed her as much as when she passed more than 50 years ago. Hector and Bubba had started to stop by more frequently. They had rapidly become very close friends. Despite this, he still mourned many people from the far past.

Hector was stopping by now with some tacos from a stand about five miles away. Brand liked all varieties of foods and especially when he could eat with company.

Hector said, "Bro, I know you like" as he pushed the container to Brand.

Hector continued, "Bubba coming. You got to see this vid. It's going blow you up!"

Brand started to grin. He always said that the five people you spend the most time with would rub off on you and you on them. So, you have to be picky about your close five. It could be their clothes, views, manners of speech, or even appearances.

Hector was learning from Brand. Always put your subject in a good mood when negotiating. Now his bringing over tacos was making sense.

As Brand was eating, he asked, "So what is so special about this video?"

Hector was now being mysterious and responded, "After you see, you will know," while he was enjoying his tacos. They were delicious and is one of the simple pleasures of the Florida. There are many great food stands that people will line up in the rain for. Such little food trucks that provide delicious meals. A Florida blessing.

Of course, Sweetbull, Brand's pit bull, had to get into the action. Hector was having none of it, but Brand had to share what seemed like half his meal.

Sweetbull was his life now that he was retired. His two children were far away, as were his two ex-wives, so the only real family that lived with him was Sweetbull. They shared all things together, especially food.

Hector had become a close friend and a great one at that. There were times they just sat together enjoying nature without saying a word. Just sitting enjoying Sweetbull and the farm in general. It was the opposite of the hard street life he had known for so long.

They were both changing, and sometimes it was better for both, as was the case here.

Lieutenant Colonel Bolt had a habit of worrying. His mind was playing out different scenarios regarding the new secure messaging systems out there. Even though Subject 9 was now using the app called Signal, which encrypts the message from point A to point B, they could still monitor transmissions. They had installed programs on Hector's, Bubba's, and Subject 9's phones and computers.

Their messages were secure. Their devices receiving them were not.

But what if they were able to get phones without Bolt's people observing it? Without the phones compromised, Hector, Bubba, and Subject 9 would be able to kept secrets.

These thoughts and many others plagued Bolt's mind. As much as he was looking forward to semi-retirement, he knew he would miss the power this job offered. Like Brand's philosophy, everything is a double edge sword. On the one hand, his worrying would be greatly reduced, but so would his power.

When Bubba arrived, the last enjoyment of food was being chewed. He had already eaten but looked disappointed that there was nothing left from Hector and Brand's feast.

Bubba started, "You all couldn't wait?" Hector responded with "Bro, you late," with a big smile while Brand just agreed with that look of his.

Hector continued, "I didn't show him anything. Know you wanted to see his face when he sees it."

At this point, Brand's curiosity was on overdrive, and he said, "Let's see this video on YouTube that's so amazing." The anticipation you could hear in his voice.

Brand had purchased an iPad with keyboard and pencil. His last iPad had died, and the size of his iPhone was too small to enjoy most things.

He had a habit of becoming very attached to his personal belongings. Whether that was his leather coat or Matilda his motorcycle. Now with his new quasi laptop, he started it up to get to the video. Only he was allowed to touch "her" for everything he loved turned into a woman.

Bubba directed him on YouTube to the site, and Brand started to watch the video. Hector and Bubba watched Brand to see first if he would notice the problem and second how he would respond.

The video was a fixed camera in a shoe store pointing to some chairs with a walkway past the chairs. The walkway abutted a full mirrored wall. There was a woman sitting and slightly moving in the chair closest to the walkway. A person walked by between the woman in the chair and the mirrored wall. That person's reflection was clearly showing in the mirror.

A few seconds later, nothing had changed with the woman. She was still slightly moving, sitting in the chair while a man dressed totally in black walked by. This time there was absolutely no reflection of the man in the mirror who had just passed by. None at all. The woman could be clearly seen. The man walking by her could be clearly seen by the naked eye, but hers was the only reflection in the mirror during the entire time.

It was obvious by Brand's focus he had seen it, and if you knew the man, you could see that he was troubled with what he had just seen.

Bubba was the first to comment, "Ain't that something? How do you think they did it?" For all of Bubba's size and mannerisms, he was smart in most things, including making money. He was a great investor. He used the internet for other projects to generate wealth. He believed it was fake and an easy way of making lots of money. He wanted us to create something similar, and we would all split the profits.

Hector believed that it was real and that we were looking at a vampire, period. Because of what they all experienced in the farmhouse, Hector wanted nothing to do with it.

Hector and Bubba were now looking at Brand to see what thoughts he had. Which side would he be on? Sometimes he would go just the opposite way you would expect. To try and predict which side he would choose was futile. The sound was so quiet within his trailer that the per-verbally pin drop could be heard.

"Wow," was all that came out. You could see his mind trying to understand how they faked it. The battle within his mind was telling. Since the farmhouse, Hector and Brand had definitely changed. They believed much more in all things they were not sure of. Bubba, on the other hand, pretty much discounted the demon aspect, thinking they had all hallucinated because of some gas or something.

There's no question that a shared experience like that either brings you together, or you'll never see each other again.

Now they were like the three musketeers, each having talents that made them collectively a force to be reckoned with. The Germans had a word for it called "gestalt." An organized whole that is perceived as more than the sum of its parts. Most importantly, they had respect and liked each other.

Bubba stated again, "Wow is all you got? How did they fake it? You think they photoshopped it and masked him out?"

Brand's reply was, "If they did, their talent is remarkable! The easiest way to resolve this is to find the fella in the video with no reflection and see for ourselves whether he is or isn't a vampire."

That's the thing about Brand, he could be so logical at times. Yes, by finding that fella and testing his reflection, all would be known. That is a lot easier said than done.

Bubba was the first to point out the flaw in his logic, "How do you plan on finding this fella?"

Brand conveyed he may have a way. They planned to meet in three days, giving Brand time to get with a friend.

Chapter 11

DARRELL'S DILEMMA

Darrell Green seemed to have everything. A beautiful wife, two children, and success in his security business, which was mostly on the electronic side.

He could never tell his wife about Subject 9 or Bolt. Even when he would meet Subject 9, he would lie to her about who he was seeing and what the meeting was about. This really bothered him, deceiving her.

He later found out that the disrupter he gave Subject 9 was defective. That also bothered him. He had interacted with Subject 9 for over seven years and had always tried to be as honest as he could. This was important to him for he was religious and believed lying to be a sin.

He felt bad providing false hope to anyone. To him, that was worse than providing no hope at all. He wanted to quit but knew he couldn't. Everything he had built would be lost. People like Bolt just don't let you quit with no consequences.

When Subject 9 called, he always answered. This time was no different.

Darrell said, "So, sir, what can I do for you?"

Brand replied, "Sorry to bother you, but there is something that really intrigues me, and I was hoping you could find some information, well, as much as you can. I have a bet, and I hope your info will win the day."

Brand also did not like to lie. In fact, he would say that you should only lie when it is most important and then sandwich it between multiple truths. That makes the person(s) receiving the lie usually believe you, but this must only be used in the most severe of times. Usually, it is just better to be truthful. Brand did not want to say he was trying to figure if this person was a vampire or not. It would sound crazy, and that would not be good. So, he broke his own rule.

Brand gave him the link to the site via a text message and said that was pretty much all he knew regarding it. Darrell, in his usual nonjudgmental way, said, no problem. He would get back to him. Brand was thinking how lucky he was to have a man like Darrell assisting him.

Lieutenant Colonel Bolt seemed to expect Darrell's call and instructed him to research it fully, and they would meet with instructions to follow.

Again, he was building his mouse trap, and this time he had a weapon that would really help Subject 9 if and when he needed. At this point, Darrell was also being observed. Not heavily but being monitored.

He had most of the information regarding the video on YouTube already on his desk. He wanted to see how much Darrell would be able to retrieve. That really was Darrell's forte. The retrieval business. Bolt went back into deep thought as was usual for him to do.

Brand was in a reflective mood. Amy had stopped texting him, so he hoped and figured she was doing good and happy with her girlfriend being back in her life.

His thoughts often went back to his first wife. If only he had been more honest and not so much a jerk. But these thoughts he did not dwell on, for he really liked to think of all the great times they had together.

At his age, thoughts of the past, 50 plus years could flood the memory by just a sound or color. If he saw someone who looked so similar to someone from his past, those fond memories stored away would come flooding back.

He looked over at Sweetbull, who was curled up on the couch. His love came pouring out. The truth was he didn't save her. She saved him!

Darrell was lucky in finding the video information. Servers, routers, and switches. Each leaves a trace, and all have detailed logs. He started by finding the original server that posted the video online, which lead to the IP address. Then he gained access to the server as a system administrator.

Each server has a master log which has the IP addresses of all computers that contacted it. From there, that provides an actual physical location. Then he contacted the owner of the shoe store acting like there was a police investigation concerning a person on the video. The shoe store clerk provided enough information for Darrell to get everything else he needed.

The truth is most people will do as you want if you approach the situation correctly. Schools now only teach two things, be quiet, as in don't ask questions and do as you are told. The trick is to make them believe you're someone of authority, and they will respond appropriately.

Now Darrell had to contact Bolt. Usually, this was done with a report, but the Lieutenant Colonel had ordered a meeting. His sense of paranoia was on fire. Lately, he hated his work for Bolt, but what could he do? He had a family to think about.

Bolt had set the meeting inside the Government building he worked at. By definition meaning it was a secure building. The process was the same as if you were going to court. After the metal detectors and guards he was led by security to meet Lieutenant Colonel Bolt.

The Lieutenant was obviously in a bad mood and abruptly said, "What have you found out?" After the briefing, Bolt had an object that was ten inches long and about two inches wide. It was in a box just big enough to hold it. It was securely wrapped in a black cloth. Darrell was instructed to give it to Subject 9 and that it would be very useful when he encounters his objective.

It was two days later that Darrell contacted Brand, which for Darrell was a long time. Like a good investigator, there are clues to find and follow. Darrell was one of the best. He not only would find information concerning the subject requested but surrounding facts that may be helpful as well. There is an art in all things, and when it came to searching for information, Darrell was a master artist.

They met at St. Armand's Circle, an upscale shopping and dining area. The traffic is always bad but once parked there are many small shops and eateries that can be traveled by foot. The allure is that in a two- or three-block area, you can pass 50 stores or more.

It has a small-town feel but is more for tourists than the locals. The shops have many esoteric items, including artwork and modern design furniture plus very stylish clothes. The restaurants are good, but everything is expensive.

Darrell had picked the area, knowing Brand liked to have company when eating. Darrell's guilt was making him change his actions. He made it a point that the lunch was on him. Darrell knew Brand was on Social Security which, without extra savings or other incomes, keeps senior citizens below the poverty level.

They picked a burger place, and the food was good even though the burgers were about $35 with sodas.

Once most of the meal was finished, Brand slowed down for there were only a few bites left. When something is really good, the last few bites need to be savored.

Darrell had a box plus his usual folder with his written report on the video. He always wrote things down, even when he was explaining things to Brand. Even if it seemed off the cuff, they were still in the report. The box was far more interesting.

Brand now could not hold back his curiosity saying, "Well, it's not my birthday or Christmas, and I assume that box is for me, so pray tell what did you bring me?"

Brand had a different way of talking to everyone he met. For some, it would be short and to the point, while for others, he seemed to use as many words as he could muster just to say something simple.

Truth was, he was trained to infiltrate any group. He could look at home in a tuxedo dinner party or hanging out with the local bikers. It was not just the clothes but learning mannerisms and then being the actor. There are times when you do this so much that you lose who you really are.

The box held a knife, but that was being generous. It was ten inches long, divided by a handle being four inches and the blade finishing the remaining six inches. The blade looked like a piece of stone. It was rough, but no one would say sharp. It looked like it was created by an amateur. It was strong but useless in a real fight against any normal knife.

To say it was disappointing was an understatement. Brand's initial excitement faded fast, but his curiosity was still there.

He began, "So you brought this to me, why?"

Now Darrell who always seemed to keep his cool, seemed a little cross and said, "Well, when you read the report, you will understand. It wasn't easy, and it seemed this...," as he moved his hand onto the box which the stone knife now rested, "...might help."

Brand always listened to the tone of the voice. Inflections can signal something other than the words being said. So, he could tell Darrell was being less patient than usual, but it seemed more than that.

Brand responded, "Brother, you know I truly appreciate all you do. Heck, I question a lot why you even bother to help me! Thanks, really!"

After the delicious but overpriced hamburgers, Brand easily took the report and stone knife back to his place. On beautiful days there was nothing nicer than riding Matilda. Once back in his rig he started to read the report, which seemed like stepping into the twilight zone.

Chapter 12

AMY'S BACK

Seeing Amy again, right at his door with no advance notice, was awesome. Her hair was longer than last time, now being the most beautiful blue he had ever seen. That and her big brown eyes and that only Amy-type smile would make anybody's day great.

She was in town and, of course, had to stop and say hello. It reminded him of people in the past, the days without personal phones. You leave the house and sometimes just stop over at someone else's house, yes, without calling or texting ahead. If they were not home, oh well.

Amy was like that, a free spirit. Maybe that is why Brand felt so comfortable with her. She came into his trailer and gave him the best hug he had ever received. She would always come in close and hug tight. This time there felt like a transferring of heartbeats. At least, that is how Brand would describe it.

Once they settled down to the business of talking, she explained that whether it was a man or woman, they all were too controlling. She laughed as she added that women were worse than men. After a while, she just wanted personal time and space.

She stated she envied his solitary existence. Being that he had already gone through most of what she was struggling with and now had at least achieved a personal peace. With that,

Brand had a big smile, saying, "Why is the grass always greener on the other side?"

Brand continued, "You have everybody wanting to be with you. I used to have that; it's wonderful! You need to be careful what you wish for!"

Amy responded with, "I got some Tequila, and I want to do old dancing."

Brand, looking at her squarely in the eyes, "I like the Tequila, but I am not jumping around like the late sixties."

Now with Amy's big eyes looking right back at him, "No, not that type. You know the way they hold each other with one arm out in front."

So after quite some drinking, they both were ready to dance.

Brand had a modified box that had a ridiculous amount of channels, over 8,000. There were movies, TV shows and music. All types of music, so after picking the right era and getting the lights into color mode, they made their way to the center of the living room.

Once her arm was holding his back and his her back their free arms came together. Brand told her to lay her head on his shoulder, and he would lead the way. As the Tequila kept kicking in and all eyes were closed, two became one. As all great things, it did not last long but was long enough that they melted into one. Each somewhere else and right where they wanted to be. The moment ended as they crashed into the table, both drunk and feeling no pain.

And in that magical moment, two souls, one young in an old body and one old in a young body. Both desiring the beauty and wisdom of the other.

Brand made a pizza, which was Amy's favorite food, but doctored it up with a ton of pepperoni and, of course, extra cheese. After the feast, which any meal with someone special becomes, it was late in the evening.

Brand would not let her leave, not until she had some sleep. Both were very drunk and the last thing Brand remembered was giving her his bedroom. He would take the couch.

When he awoke, he was in his bedroom, and Amy was gone. Sweetbull was just staring at him with an expression that outside was needed now. As he arrived in the living room, Amy had cleaned up most of the mess made the night before. He noticed a note on the table which said, "Till Next Time," with a smiley face.

Brand knew she would be gone and yet he also knew that some time in the future she would drop back in again. She reminded him of his little gypsie, magical and mysterious but can never be contained.

He thought of a joke that seemed so true. There was a man who met a Genie. The Genie gave him one wish. The man said he wanted a road to Hawaii. The Genie looked stressed and said, that's really hard. How about something else. The man thought a bit and said he wanted to understand women. The Genie replied do you want one or two lanes.

For all the time Brand had spent studying human nature, women were a complete mystery.

Tomorrow he would have to meet up with Hector and Bubba to go over his plan to catch the vampire.

Chapter 13

THE PLAN

The next day Hector and Bubba came over to find out what Brand had discovered about the video. This time there was no food being eaten.

The rig had two couches and two lazy boy chairs in front of the television. The kitchen table fit two comfortably, with Brand on one side and Hector on the other. Bubba had picked one of the couches, but all eyes were on Brand.

Brand started with, "The man in the video's name is Gabriel Hand. Yea, I know how it sounds, but that's his name."

Brand continued, "The good news is he is located in Miami, and I even have his general routine." He waited there to see what response he would receive.

Hector started with, "Bro, what's your plan? Sounds like you want us to do a road trip."

Before Bubba could speak, Brand shouted, he would say spoke loudly, "Exactly, I have a plan that will not only get us our answer but make us all money!"

After hearing the details, Bubba was not happy with the plan, but he had to admit he was the right man for the job, at least compared to Hector.

Bubba started, "So Hector and I go down there cause your too busy to go. There's a street he travels to every day, usually around 6:00 p.m. He always wears black with a black hat. It's a bad part of town, and I am supposed to find him and walk up to him holding a mirror that's covered. Hector will be on the other side with his camera zoomed in while I pull the cover from the mirror, and Hector captures it all on video."

At that point, Brand said loudly, "Exactly! Either his shadow will show up or not. If his shadow does not, we have a great video to show on YouTube. And if it does, we can use it to debunk the original we saw. Either way, it will be worth some money."

Bubba was still upset, "Why aren't you going to be there?" At this Brand looked seriously in Bubba's eyes and said, "I told you I have other business to take care of."

Brand did not go over most of the information within the report. Nor did he show the knife he was given by Darrell. If you could call it a knife. It was more like a stone carved in the shape of a knife. He had his reasons for not going, which were revealed later.

Plato said, "It is only the dead who have seen the end of the war." How true that is today as when it was said. For the simple battle of survival, is that not a war and is there anything simple about it?

Brand's thoughts pondered on so many things. He could be so detached that he would love you and never speak to you again.

He thought of Sweetbull and how she loved to meet new people. Demanding she kiss them on the face and being so excited to be with them. Rarely does she show that excitement to Brand, only when he has been away on a job and then comes home to find that outpouring of affection. She shows love all the time when Brand is home but in a different way. A more subtle way.

It reminded him of his relationship with God. Here the Lord provides all that he needs, like he does for Sweetbull, but he still is always looking for that one special lady when he should really just be content to love and have the love of the Lord.

At a certain age, that not only becomes enough, it is more than enough. There still was a lot of planning to do for Bubba and Hector's trip. And the fact that he had not been totally honest was weighing on him. He had not lied, but he had withheld some truths. That made him feel all the more lousy.

He turned to look at Sweetbull, but she was curled up tight. He smiled to himself. At least someone was going to sleep well.

He was working on the plan for Bubba and Hector's Miami trip. While doing this, he received a text from an old friend, Perry, who said she missed him. Brand was loving his new iPad and the way it made him feel connected to people and the world.

Brand thought that saying you miss someone is one of the nicest things that can be said. It makes people feel good, being missed.

They made plans to meet sometime soon for one of their Chinese buffet lunches. He loved her in his own way, always wishing her happiness and peace.

He remembered their last buffet lunch, they had so much fun talking about everything. He always left so full it was hard to walk. He spoke to himself, saying, yes, as soon as this adventure with Bubba and Hector is over, it is lunch with Perry!

Chapter 14

GABRIEL HAND

The vampire they were seeking had established habits which Brand knew meant either he was very confident regarding his survival or just did not care who was watching. Brand's instinct was for the former and felt that would be his Achilles' heel. It would allow Bubba to get close while Hector would be able to record the whole event.

By the time Bubba and Hector left in Bubba's new truck, Brand was already gone. They had stopped by even though all the information was sent to their phones. Whatever the reason they stopped by, Brand's Matilda was absent, and he had said in his instructions not to call or text him for he would not be able to respond.

Bubba was in a road trip mood while Hector was more concerned about what they were going to do. They were to get there a day before and scout out the street but to be done by 4:00 p.m. and no later. The filming would take place the next day at 6:00 p.m.

They decided first to get a room and after that the reconnaissance. Then they would go back to the room to freshen up. Then off to the clubs. Nothing like having a plan.

Most places are somewhat similar except for the edges. Those special places or things that a town or city has. Perhaps they are the Broadway shows, scenic views, or famous landmarks. However, with the highs come the lows. Places not talked about except if your needs place you there.

The street that Bubba and Hector were heading for was lined with the saddest and worst elements of any place. The junkies with their connections. The beggars who had reached the bottom and somehow kept going down. The working women and the poorest of the poor trying to survive and re-group.

It was a place that thrived on sadness and only emitted bad luck, where the darkness was everywhere and suffocating. A place you would not venture without a good reason.

Gabriel Hand was not his real name. He looked like someone in their late twenties. He had black hair that curled a bit with very pale skin coloring. There was no mercy in his eyes. His lips had a natural reddish look with a strong jawline ending in a square chin.

Long-life provides its own rewards but also has its down-sides. How long can you use a name before it has too much history? Before your friends start to realize that in 20 years you haven't changed. Even the closest become jealous of wealth and possessions, but nothing compares to eternal life.

How many would give how much to have their lives forever extended?

But it is not that you feel you live forever, just that every-thing else around you disappears into death. For even in the brief time of a thousand years how much has been lost? Not just lost but completely forgotten.

If people knew Gabriel's history, they would classify it as horrific. Death clung to him. It was like a bloodstain on your favorite clothes. Try as you may to remove the stain there are times when it only becomes more embedded into the fabric.

Black was his color of choice. When you have to kill to live, and you have centuries of doing it, maybe it reflects what we would call the color of his soul. But make no mistake, Gabriel

Hand had no soul, and no one really knows why he dressed that way.

Throughout the years many atrocities happened, and many were forgotten. Perhaps there were no survivors. Or the few who survived left no recordings of its passage. Sometimes it is the victor who eliminated all traces of the event.

Gabriel Hand was more aware of acts of atrocities than any other person on the planet. That is not surprising, for Gabriel was not human, and he caused so much of the suffering. Whether it was 200 years ago as he terrorized villages or 2,000 years ago, he never was stopped.

Sometimes an entire army would go after just him and not only fail but lose most of the army with the ones left only speaking of terrors that should never be mentioned.

The villages he terrorized. The small colonies that seemed to disappear of all human life overnight. The posters of missing people.

He had become so strong and nonchalant that he did not worry about hiding from the law.

The type of vampire Gabriel was he not only enjoyed drinking blood, but he had very strong preferences, such as liking to scare his victims. He would say that it made their blood so much more potent and delicious. In that regard, the younger the blood, the better overall its properties that Gabriel preferred.

Unknown to many, there are more than just four types of blood. Even the four types have many different properties. Gabriel enjoyed the most pure innocent blood, which almost always has to be from a child.

If some men leave a trail of blood, then Gabriel left a river.

Gabriel needed to live, and humans were his food. It was as simple as that to him. He was the superior and they the cattle.

His true interest may never be known, but his last meal was someone that others cared greatly about.

Lieutenant Colonel Bolt had many connections from politicians, police, military, spies, company CEOs, and others of great importance. Many sensitive issues came across his desk, and hard decisions at times needed to be made.

Today the folder of Gabriel Hand was on his desk. The facts were clear. How to proceed was the pressing question. Vampires are not portrayed correctly in the movies. More specifically, there are different types, with some having unique capabilities. Gabriel Hand was the most malevolent type. That he is tolerated is because of the possible potential downside if things go wrong in containing or termination.

Like when an insurance company will pay $10,000 for a slip and fall compared to going to court and possibly losing millions. It's a win from the insurance company's standpoint, even though they just lost $10,000.

Bolt had already started to mess with Gabriel Hand's life. He had his undercover agent contact Bubba clandestinely about the video of Gabriel at the shoe store, planting the seed that a lot of money could be made. It was assumed Bubba would contact Hector or Subject 9. That assumption paid off.

Bolt couldn't explain it, but he felt like he knew how things would happen before their actual outcome. He had rightly assumed. Subject 9 would get involved, and again he was right. Things were going well. He did not have a clear picture yet how it would all turn out.

The knife should be a big help as it was very hard for him to attain. Not only did he have to call in a big favor, but the attainment was very difficult. The previous owner of the knife did not let it go willingly.

One last thought Lieutenant Colonel Bolt had was that Subject 9 had a way of surviving. A way of bringing bad luck to his enemies or having just the right coincidences fall his way. Subject 9 versus Gabriel Hand would soon put that survival luck to the ultimate test.

When Bubba and Hector checked out the street, they were taken aback. Both were carrying weapons, specifically guns and a knife backup, besides each other for protection. Yet, they were uneasy and did not want to split up. Bubba was staying on the walkway while Hector crossed the road to the gravel path.

They had to split up and do some video tests because, in reality, who knows how this will turn out. To both, it seemed more and more like a crazy plan with Brand nowhere to be found.

Times like that are found on boats or men lost in the deserts or jungles of the world. When you're scared, you tend to turn on whoever is not there with you or who sent you or each other. Brand was guilty of two of three.

When they first started walking the street, they were asked what they wanted. Girls, drugs, or maybe something else? One woman started rubbing Bubba in places a proper lady would not do in public. Hector was grabbed by a beggar for some change right above his knee, pretty fiercely. Hector had almost pulled his gun when Bubba pushed his hand back to his body. Then with sudden aggression, Bubba yelled at the beggar to be gone, or he would break him in two and to never touch his friend again.

The beggar scattered away as Bubba and Hector also wanted to leave. After their adrenaline had settled, they searched for the best place to expose this "fella." Bubba and Hector were now ready for the best part of the trip. Miami nightlife.

There's a charge in the air when you know something big is just about to happen. It is like everything becomes more real. Sounds become more distinct. Colors have more shades. Even the air feels and smells more alive.

One can feel their heartbeat and their blood flow. The excitement just before the event. That feeling pulsing through your body is addictive.

Truth was Bubba, Hector, and Brand all craved that feeling. If you survive, then you really know you're alive. It was one of the bonds that made them the three musketeers, as they liked to think of themselves.

Bubba and Hector were there by 5:30 p.m. Neither had slept particularly well, but their adrenaline was high. When on a mission like this, it is hard to be tired. You know the whole event will be done within a minute at most, but how smoothly it will exactly transpire, well, nobody really knows. That's part of the excitement or rush that is felt.

Just as predicted, Gabriel was walking right to them. Bubba was in his spot. The area they had previously scouted that was the most optimal. Hector was across the street with his phone ready to record. All Bubba had to do was wait and then step in front of him to slow him down while pulling the cover off the mirror. The mirror was two feet wide by three feet tall. Not hard for Bubba to handle with relative ease in one arm.

Gabriel seemed totally relaxed and oblivious to his surroundings. Like a true hunter at the top of his game. He has no fear of the presence of others.

Bubba was not just big but agile and played his part to perfection. He pulled the cloth off while acting like he was now going to cross the street. That happened just as Gabriel was passing by him. Hector was ready and already recording the event.

What happened next was fast and unexpected. Gabriel was now instantly aware of almost all that was around him. He pushed Bubba with his left hand with such force that the mirror broke and Bubba fell down. Given Bubba's size that was not easy to do, and it happened within a second. Gabriel crossed the street so fast that literally just one more second went by, and he ripped the phone from Hector's hand. As quick as he had appeared, he was gone. Whichever way he went was unknown, but the aftermath was Hector regaining his composure and going to see if Bubba was okay.

By the time he crossed the street, the beggar was helping Bubba. Bubba was not really hurt but discombobulated.

After the beggar said something to Bubba, he smiled brightly, saying, "I knew it, I knew you'd be here."

Hector was now getting upset about the loss of his phone since Bubba seemed okay.

Then the beggar looked at Hector and said, "It's only a phone. We got the video on my iPhone."

Next the beggar gave a big grin, and Hector was shaking his head, now smiling, "Bro, you too much!"

Brand said, "Let's go home, and I will explain everything." The three musketeers were back together with video in hand.

Once back at Brand's rig, there were questions that needed answers, and so Brand began.

"Some of the information I received made it, so I had to keep things secret. Gabriel can read minds only when he is within three feet of his subject. That is why I provided only what you needed to know. If you knew I would be there, we would have lost an advantage on him."

Now Bubba started, "If he can read minds, by you being there, he could have just read yours anyhow!"

Brand replied, "You're right. If he had come within three feet of me, but Gabriel is arrogant. The fact he keeps the same pattern shows he feels omnipotent, so I figured with my disguise he would not be concerned."

Brand continued, "The fact is that we do and don't observe many things all at the same time. The brain is trained to pick up the unusual and to ignore the common. I rest my case on the fact that Hector almost shot me when I pulled his leg," ending with a big smile.

Now the video that was on Brand's iPhone was reviewed. Everything happened so fast that the camera barely recorded anything. When the cloth fell of the mirror, Gabriel's hand moved so fast that it was really hard to tell if there was a reflection or not. Then Gabriel moved so fast again that the camera didn't show his moments.

Brand was across the street and was slightly adjacent of Hector before Bubba had pulled the cloth from the mirror, but even there, he barely got any video let alone good video.

After the viewing Brand continued, "I read the information I was given but truly had a hard time believing it was true. Now I know it is!"

Bolt was being briefed on the events regarding Subject 9 and Gabriel Hand. He really didn't know what to expect to happen and was currently doing things against procedures he himself had put into place. But his instincts were on fire, telling him to just monitor. No current action should be implemented. At his age, after a lifetime trusting his instincts, he instructed his agents to continue to monitor and contact him if any major changes occurred.

Brand looked troubled, which was not a usual look. Like a speaker that has been heckled and becomes a bit discombobulated before regaining his composure. Really though, it was more than that. He was troubled for putting his friends in danger and knowing much more trouble was coming.

Brand started by saying, "I am sorry for putting you guys in danger. You have to admit, unless Gabriel is seen, it is hard to believe he is a real vampire."

He continued, "What comes next I cannot get you involved in. It's best not to say anything else! Thank you, and I'm sorry the video turned out so bad."

Hector was first and forceful, "Bro you have a death wish! All you talk about is a warrior's death. All three of us could not stop him! Let it go! We're lucky to be alive, and I am going to stay that way!"

Bubba, who was in good spirits, changed suddenly and said, "How will you go about it?"

Brand responded, "Can't risk that Gabriel will get within three feet of you and know everything. If you want to know, you will have to stay here day and night and until it happens."

Bubba had no desire to die in any way, warrior's death included. Truth always was that Brand was the true fighter in the group.

Bubba then said, "I don't like to be pushed. I am with you. Gabriel, I owe you!"

Brand was very serious during this whole time. He was not directly looking at Bubba but at Hector. He had seen that look on men in battle. They would rather be shot than do what is going to be needed to be done. Brand had no desire to have Hector go through this. Heck, he did not want Bubba to help. The chance of success was very low, and death on the other side of the scale, extremely high.

Brand said, "Hector, there is no shame. You're a good man-"

Before he could continue, Hector shouted, "I'm in! Just think you're all crazy!"

Most would not understand why two people would do something they most certainly don't want to do.

The Roman army was one of the greatest forces the world had seen. They conquered a vast part of their known world because they fought to the last man. There never was a surrender. If they lost the battalion, more soldiers would arrive from Rome.

The slogan, "Come home with your shield or on your shield," was the norm. If a soldier ran away from the battle, someone within his group would be killed. Of course, they would also kill the deserter when found. To leave, if even successful, meant one of your friends will die.

Brand understood why these two men who wanted nothing to do with this operation were still willing to try, even if it meant death. When you become a unit, and you rely on each other, you are one for all and all for one. They truly had merged not just as friends but as a team, and you don't leave anyone behind in the battle.

Brand was struck with great emotions over all that had just transpired. He suggested they all get a good night sleep and, in the morning, he would reveal all the information he had about Gabriel. Then they would go over his plan on how to defeat him.

Chapter 15

REGROUP

Florida is not called the sunshine state for nothing. Another beautiful Floridian day had arrived. The locals are very picky about their weather. A few too many clouds or three to four degrees above or below what one thinks is perfect will give the day an unfavorable rating.

Last night's adventure seemed far away to Bubba, but Hector was sorely missing his phone. Brand was all inside himself with Bubba taking care of Sweetbull.

Bubba was a businessman and very shrewd when it came to making money. He had a website that sold merchandise he peddled from his YouTube channel. As all good businessmen do, he was diversified and had funneled the early profits from YouTube to the stock market. Bubba knew that to really make money, you have to have other people make it for you. In that way, whether you're on vacation or sleeping, you're still making money. Bubba always seemed to have more money than he needed. Unlike Hector and Brand.

Hector was troubled by the loss of his phone and not being able to make any money for the next week. Brand never had more than two days of food in his rig and was always tight on money.

Bubba, who had more class than any rich person to be seen, just said, "Me and Hector are going to get some supplies and then hear all the stuff plus your plan." With that and a smile, they were off.

When they arrived back at Brand's rig, Hector was all smiles with his new phone, plus Brand saw more food than he thought could be stored in his kitchen.

Before he could say anything, Bubba said, "My treat. We have to be ready for Gabe, and that's not doable on an empty belly."

Brand not only relayed what was in the report but also handed it to them for their review. Then he showed them the knife that was given to him, which also was mentioned amongst the paperwork.

"So, you see by the report, unless Gabriel is actually seen, it's really hard to believe," Brand said, still feeling guilty about not sharing all he knew from the start.

"Again, Hector and Bubba, you can walk away right now. I'll be fine!"

Bubba looked at Hector with a look of told you so. Then Hector said, "No, bro, we'll be fine. Now, what's the plan?"

Every advantage also becomes a disadvantage, so would begin the plan to contain Gabriel Hand. This man was at least 2,000 years old. He did not like sunlight. That is not to say it would kill him, but it was a great annoyance. He had perfected staying anonymous and moving at great speeds.

The report Darrell had provided mentioned that the knife is greatly valued by Gabriel and, at all costs, should not be transferred into his possession.

This part of the report intrigued Brand. It just said greatly valued. Why would Gabriel Hand value a stone knife so badly?

In Brand's mind, there were two reasons to place such a high value. One would be that it is so extraordinary, such a one of a kind, that whoever possesses it must gain some type of power! Or two, it is something that can hurt Gabriel, and by Gabriel possessing it, he would have control over its use.

Brand was hoping it was the latter. His secret weapon. Once Hector and Bubba knew all the facts, they could wait no longer to hear the plan.

Brand loved history of all types. *The Art of War* by Sun Tzu is a must-read for anyone at war. And is not daily living a battle of survival. This book often gave him inspiration in trying times.

"We have lost the advantage of surprise, but we are going to pick the place and the time. In the teachings of *The Art of War*, the more of these elements we control, the greater the advantage should go our way in any engagement."

Now Hector started, "Bro, how we going to get him in a place and time we want?" Bubba shaking his head up and down in agreement to the last question by Hector.

Brand had that smile, the cat that ate the canary look and said, "There's a farm about twenty miles from here that's abandoned. That's where we set the trap and have Gabriel come to us. Where and when we want. Then finish his campaign of terror."

Now his audience was silent. Brand would be in front of a very deep trench, say 4 feet wide by 10 feet long and as deep as possible. It would have a quick, sand-like substance at the bottom and the top camouflaged, ready for Gabriel to fall into.

Hector jumping in again, "Bro, how we going to get him to that spot?"

Brand said, "I have his phone number. I am going to call and convince him to come."

Again, with that sly smile, "But first, we have to set the trap."

Brand would be the bait, and once Gabriel fell into the pit, Bubba would shoot him to slow him down. Then they would fill it with cement to permanently stop him.

Brand continued, "His speed should be nullified within the pit while shooting him will slow him down. It may work!"

Now Bubba spoke up, "Where are we going to get a backhoe, not to mention all of the other stuff like cement? Who's going to mix up this quick sand stuff?"

Brand continued, "Roy has a backhoe here, and I will make something up for the reason why I need it. I am sure he will help. He is quite skilled in using a backhoe. What I need won't take him long to do. Your right about the quick sand mix and setting up the camouflage. It's a plan. A work in progress."

Brand now looked at his friends. They were more than friends at this point. They were family. He said, "I truly appreciate your being there, but I will be fine. You guys can be located close but out of danger."

Bubba would have none of it, saying, "Sounds good, but I'll have your back when you're standing in front of the pit."

Brand did not share the battle that raged within his mind. Did he have a death wish? He was thinking back to his impulsive fight with Tiny. Now he felt it was his destiny, win or lose, to compete with Gabriel. Deep down, he knew his plan had a one in a million chance of success. Now he really did not want Bubba and Hector there, but he couldn't stop them either.

One side of him was arguing that the evil Gabriel had done and still was causing had to be stopped. Even if he only had a one-in-a-million chance, it was worth taking it to stop this type of depravity. Brand was thinking that his own mortality would be within a ten-year time, naturally at best. It was worth the chance.

The other side of him was saying just let it go. Your curiosity had put Hector and Bubba in jeopardy already. How could he stop a creature so old and so tough that armies could not stop him? This was all crazy, and he needed to back away.

After talking with Roy on the phone, he said he would get back to Brand. Brand felt Roy seemed very distant and noncommittal. In reality, most of the plan would lie in having Roy's help. If anyone could make a quick sand mix within a trench that has a camouflage cover, it was Roy.

Brand looked at the sky like fate would answer his question. If Roy helped, it was fate saying this is your destiny. If Roy did not help, then maybe this fight should be left to another.

Bolt was getting old. At 66, that's how it felt to him. Of course, to most, that is definitely old. Maybe that is why he was doing things concerning Subject 9 in a looser manner.

With less time ahead, things seemed like they needed to speed up in finding out the true powers of RBs. He also related closer to Subject 9 than the others subjects. Their age was similar, and he had monitored him for so long.

He instructed Roy to transport his backhoe to the site, but Bolt would send a specialized team to prepare the trap.

One thing about the military, they had huge resources and great knowledge regarding many things.

Fate is a fickle but a funny thing. Deep down, both Lieutenant Colonel Bolt and Brand Wright had an unexplainable hatred for Gabriel Hand. Like when some people have a fear of spiders or snakes, even when they have never been hurt by them. Both wanted Gabriel dead without voicing that feeling out loud. Subconsciously they were on a parallel path, almost working together to clean the planet of Gabriel. Both knowing that this may be the greatest thing they have ever done for mankind.

Florida's weather, unlike the grey skies of Philadelphia, was mostly always blue with just a few clouds. It could even rain in Florida without a cloud in the sky. The weather was uplifting. After the call he had just received from Roy, Brand was optimistic the plan might work.

He really wanted Hector and Bubba to stay back from the action. Hector he would demand to stay away to *help* them in some way. But Bubba, he could see, really wanted to help, and denying him his spot would not be right.

Each man has the right to make his own choice on where his last stand may be. If Bubba wanted to be next to Brand, then he was honored to have him there.

For Brand most of the time, he thought in a warrior's way. It is a code that becomes who you are. So, at this moment, plans were turning into actions. Roy said it would take about two to three days for it to be right. He said he was an expert in these things. How fortuitous that was, or was it a sign that the universe wanted to see this moment played out.

Roy was more than willing to help. He asked for no money and acted like he knew exactly how to complete it.

How luckier could Brand get than that. Deep down though Brand felt that there must be something else going on below the surface.

Brand had a pre-paid phone for times that called for more security than a personal phone would provide. He only had one chance to get it right with his phone call to Gabriel. He needed to take charge in controlling the conversation. Clear on his demands and ending it on his terms.

Roy had taken the backhoe as requested by Bolt, but it was not needed because Bolt's team was already there surveying the grounds and had brought their own equipment. Most of the time, we never get to see close-up our tax dollars at work. If you had the privilege of seeing that team locate the best place and design for the trap required, it was impressive.

Ground surveys, in addition to many bags of chemicals, tubing, and a variety of other things assembled. Men wearing hard hats and scientific-looking people discussed the project at hand. Most impressive was the speed at which the completion and design of the trap occurred. When it was finished they had installed chicken wire around the perimeter for the trap was invisible to see.

Brand had planned for the event to happen tomorrow, so the phone call to Gabriel had to be made today. This was key to the whole plan, and it rested on his shoulders. He wanted the trap ready before the call so the time would be short after they talked before their final meeting.

Because make no mistake, someone was not going home after they met.

Chapter 16

THE CALL

Brand made the phone call at 5:45 p.m., hoping it was a good time for Gabriel to answer. Gabriel usually was walking the street by 6:00 p.m. To his surprise and prayers, it was answered on the first ring.

"Yes" was all that was said by Gabriel.

Sometimes in life, you're given just one chance to hit the bullseye. If he stumbled here, there would be no second chance to get him to the trap.

Brand replied, "I know all about you. You're not as anonymous as you think. I have videos of you in action, and I want $500,000. If you don't meet me at high noon tomorrow at the location that I will text, then I will make you a superstar! Everyone will be looking for you!"

At first, nothing. Then, "Goodbye," was heard from Gabriel. At that moment, Brand had texted him a picture of the stone knife.

Brand said firmly, "Check the picture I just texted you. I know you want it. I will sweeten the deal. Bring the money, and I'll give you the knife. Understand, though, that if you're later than 12:00 p.m., the deal is off, and believe me, you will never find me. I know how to be anonymous!"

Again silence. Then, "Send me the location. Goodbye." Brand quickly sent the location via text, which at times can be such a wonderful thing if not overused. Brand was surprised at how polite Gabriel was. He figured the knife was the only thing that would make Gabriel bow to his demands. But he had to make it look like just someone hungry for money.

Tomorrow was going to be a big day. Maybe his last day. So Sweetbull got even better food than usual, Brand not being hungry. She also got more kisses than usual that night. Knowing you could very well die tomorrow makes everything so special the night before.

Early the next morning Brand was out with Sweetbull doing their first walk. Roy walked over to Brand with a serious look. That was quite an unusual look for Roy to have.

Roy started off by saying, "I have set up what you wanted for the most part. Be careful as it is very dangerous. I would be happy to be there with you. I think you might need some help."

Brand was touched, saying, "Thank you, my friend, really. Of course, you are always a big help with everything, but honestly, I wish Bubba and Hector would not be there."

Then something happened that had never happened before. Roy bent down and wrapped his huge arms around Brand gently. Brand gave a hug back. Roy whispered, "Be careful, my friend."

Roy, Brand, Hector, and Bubba all loaded into Bubba's truck and headed to the abandoned farm to see the results of Roy's trap. They needed to know how to operate the trap with the cement once the trap was sprung.

Brand's thoughts were now having doubts about how all this would go down. Again, he tried before they got in the truck, to no avail, to get Bubba and Hector both out of danger's way.

First impressions upon seeing the farmhouse and path that led to the front door were unimpressive. There was a farmhouse with a porch. It seemed all farmhouses had them. There were three steps from the dirt to the porch's wood floor. Before the porch's steps was a scattered grass path that had what were once white rocks about 4 feet apart on each side. It all had seen better days but looked completely normal.

Hector was the first to say what was on everyone's mind, "Did you make da trap?" Then as they got closer, for it was a good thirty yards from the turn off the road, they saw the chicken wire that surrounded the trap.

Roy's work was amazing. Power was running in the farmhouse, and he explained what he had set up. The trap itself was an oval, almost being a perfect circle. Roy explained that design makes the quicksand work better.

Also, he did not set it up with cement but had installed jets within the trap that will shoot a liquid cement or actually more like glue. The advantage being it hardened much faster. He was adamant that no one should be near the trap when it was activated. The quicksand was very dangerous, and no one should go into the trap for any reason.

Within the farmhouse by the window was what looked like Scuba tanks around a central tank with the main pipe leading from it going through the floor and disappearing from there. There was a cable with a box attached that had one toggle switch with down doing nothing and up activating the liquid glue jets.

Hector would man the window and activate the switch when needed. Brand had talked with Hector telling him under NO circumstances was he to activate the switch without Brand saying so.

There were about 4 feet from the porch to the trap. That was where Brand would make his stand with Bubba on the porch backing him up.

They all rode back to Brand's rig and contemplated what was to come next.

Brand wanted to go back to the farmhouse by 10:00 a.m., this time begging Bubba and Hector to stay here at his rig, to please sit this one out. If they had second thoughts to their credit, they did not show it. Brand remembered a friend who had his first experience being in prison.

His friend declaring, “It's not real until it's real, and then it's really real.” That quote always made him smile even now when it was going from not real to real. Soon to really real, but what's after that?

Chapter 17

LAST STAND

They went in Bubba's truck which was nicely fitted with a winch in the front, double tires in the back with oversized wheels, and was also about two feet higher from the ground than it had any right to be.

It was parked on the left side of the farmhouse with the front slightly angled facing the trap. They had removed the chicken wire around the trap, which they called the pit, and everybody was starting to relax as they had another hour and a half before high noon.

Hector was in the farmhouse by the front window, as Brand did not want Gabriel to see him if he arrived early. Bubba and Brand were sitting on the steps of the porch. From the trap to the steps of the porch, there were about 4 feet. That would be Brand's stage!

Brand had been smoking more and was chain-smoking at this point. It had become a beautiful Florida day, maybe a bit too hot, but it felt good to Brand. You could see the main road from the porch on both sides except for a bit in the front due to trees. The show was about to begin.

A black car came racing up the road, seemingly out of place, for it was moving too fast. The windows were as dark as the black paint on their frame. Even the front window was a darker shade than Brand had ever seen. Gabriel came to do business.

It whipped around the turn leading to the entrance of the farmhouse property. Then it stopped abruptly about 10 feet before the walkway to the porch. There were about 20 feet before the beginning of the trap, with another 4 feet after to the steps of the porch. The door slowly opened, which was in stark contrast to how quickly the car had approached.

Imagine going to work not for 40 years but for over 2,000 years. You drive sometimes through bad weather, see terrible accidents occasionally, have car problems and other annoyances to deal with each day. And yet, for 40 years, you survive. No matter how big or annoying, nothing has stopped you from surviving. Now imagine that for 2,000 years.

Gabriel had good reasons to be overconfident. Brand's whole plan relied on it. However, someone like Gabriel lived by instinct. Who knew what those dark eyes could see and what terrible plans he had in his mind to do to those who threatened his existence?

Gabriel started to walk the path to the front porch. At the same time, Brand had walked down from the porch and was on his 4-foot square before the trap. Bubba, who was supposed to stay on the porch, had walked down slightly adjacent behind Brand.

Gabriel seemed like a cat being careful of every step but still slowly coming right to them and the trap. It was at 3 or 4 feet before the beginning of the trap when he stopped. He still hadn't said a word but just stopped.

Now Brand was looking at Gabriel. They were about 12 feet apart, both with cold stares at the other. Brand was always good at getting people to respond. Saying something that he knew would get a reaction. Didn't matter what the reaction was. Once the person responded to it, Brand felt like he won.

Brand started, "So this is the bad Gabriel Hand. Wow. I am less than impressed. Are you scared of an old man? I am not like the children you scare so easily?"

Still nothing. All he wanted was for Gabriel to take a few more steps forward. Nothing.

Brand started again but this time making a critical mistake. As he was speaking to Gabriel, he slightly turned his body towards Bubba taking his eyes off his opponent.

"Wow, Bubba, take a video of this. I want to enjoy this moment many..."

At that moment, Gabriel moved with the quickness and agility of a cat. He had taken three steps. If just one more step, he would have met the trap. That is when he started his leap towards Brand's throat with his hands that were now more like claws. By the time Brand had swiveled back to look at Gabriel, they were about two feet apart, with Brand seeing Gabriel but being frozen and unable to move or respond.

Gabriel should have completed the death blow with his right hand that was more like a claw with fingernails resembling the sharpness of razors.

From Brand's perspective, everything slowed down, and it was like a minute within a second. Gabriel had easily jumped the 8-foot trap and was a swipe away from killing him. At the same moment, Bubba had appeared and gave Gabriel a shoulder block which seemed like they were both frozen in time. Then everything sped up again, and Bubba went flying backward, as Gabriel's horizontal momentum disappeared and his knees hit the trap.

Now Gabriel was half in the trap, and half out with his right claw hand dug into the dirt about 2 inches from the trap's entrance, and his left hand had just grabbed Bubba's foot.

Then a second later, Gabriel's right hand wedged in the dirt was gone as the dirt caved back into the trap. The dirt and Gabriel had disappeared into the trap. Less than a second later, Bubba went flying behind Gabriel as his left clawed hand on Bubba's foot never let go.

Bubba had never taken his eyes off Gabriel, so when Gabriel had started his move, Bubba also started moving to block him. Brand's life was saved because of Bubba's focus and response to what he saw. Bubba would later say Gabriel seemed a bit slower than the previous time they met.

Brand pulled the stone knife out, which was seated by his belt buckle and without a second wasted jumped into the trap. Both hands extended in front with the stone knife extended down, falling into the trap like a missile looking for its target.

Lieutenant Colonel Bolt had been watching the monitors intensely as others also were doing. Bolt was angry with himself. What did he expect to happen? What he did not expect was Subject 9 to fight Gabriel hand to hand. He was angry in breaking his own rules and losing Subject 9.

Just then, the phone rang with Bolt answering, "No, don't turn on the shower. Just monitor." Yes, sir, was the answer.

The shower was the so-called liquid cement, but in reality, it was much worse than that.

Bolt had to give Subject 9 credit. He had guts. Only a few men would jump into certain death. Bolt having combat experience, knew that what was happening on the ground could be total unclear to command. Even though he had multiple angles and an up-close live video, he could not see into the trap. He would give Subject 9 the benefit of the doubt, but he was expecting Gabriel to claw his way out.

Gabriel had thrown Bubba behind him as they both went into the trap. The quicksand mix was more effective than Brand had expected. As Brand went to stab Gabriel, he had raised his head instinctively, knowing danger was coming. Unfortunately for Gabriel, that was the last sight his right eye would ever see. His scream of pain was bone-chilling, and at the same time, he shifted his foot, bringing the quicksand to his chest.

Bubba, now regaining his senses, pulled his gun out and shot Gabriel in the back. Luckily for Brand, no bullets had gone straight thru. Bubba had empty six rounds that had only made Gabriel angrier. In doing so, Bubba had now sunken to his shoulders with both arms below his head.

Brand now acted on instinct himself. Something told him the stone knife needed to be in Gabriel's heart. So right after the last round from Bubba went into Gabriel's back, Brand pulled the stone knife from Gabriel's right eye socket and drove it into his chest bone. Brand thought he might not be able to pierce it, but it went right in with no problem. Brand then turned his hand like he was opening a doorknob, turning the nasty knife in a circular motion through Gabriel's heart.

Within five seconds of that, Gabriel turned into dust. A black powder that seemed to explode and then was gone. After a second or two of that shock, Brand looked at Bubba, who was chin high in quicksand.

Brand had also sunken with his shoulders being above the quicksand. One arm deep within the quicksand mix and the other near his head with his new most prized possession, the knife. He instantly knew it was more than just a knife. It had changed form once Gabriel's body exploded.

Now it was longer with a cutting edge on both sides resembling a short Roman sword, but the blade was polished in a way that resembled a black glass mirror having reflective properties. It was sharper than a razor, and he felt it was best never to touch the blade as it will always cut its target. The handle still had a stone look but now was granite having black, grey, and white colors with finger inlays for its owner. The granite looked old but had a remarkable cleanness to it. Like no substance could stain it, for that matter, the blade also was perfectly clean. It had a thumb guard that had a triangle shape so that the opposing weapon would run off it.

Its change was unbelievable and awesome at the same time. Brand instantly had many thoughts that seemed to know all about this new weapon, but weapon was not the right term. He sensed that it was alive, having feelings and desires. Also that it had a vast knowledge of so many things over a period of time that cannot be imagined by a human existence.

Brand seemed lost in thoughts but Bubba was sinking lower, and actions needed to happen.

"Hector, help!" was all Brand could yell, and he did this with all he had in him.

Bolt's phone again rang, "Sir, do you want us to do a clean-up?"

The answer was short, "No. Keep monitoring"

Poor Hector was in the farmhouse and had seen all that had taken place. The seconds before Brand's yell were pure agony for him. He fought with his mind about pushing the switch up, maybe Brand and Bubba were already gone, and this might be the only thing to stop Gabriel. The other side of his mind was saying Brand said not to do it unless he gave the order. He was truly grateful to hear his name and dropped the box before running to his friends in trouble.

Bubba was up to his neck in the quicksand, but it was like a mix of quicksand and cement. Any little movement sent you lower and seemed to hold you tighter.

Brand yelled, "Use the winch on the truck," which Hector did directly. Hector put the winch into a free spin and hauled the end, dropping it into the trap directly in front of Brand.

Brand could have dropped the short sword to grab the winch, instead he yelled to Hector to rethrow it directly to Bubba.

There was a bond between him and the entity, and he would never put it into danger. Again time seemed to slow down and what seemed like a thousand thoughts entered and was processed by his mind.

Bubba had both arms in the quicksand but was able to free them and grab the winch's hook. Hector then started the winch's motor pulling Bubba to safety.

Hector then repeated the process landing the hook right near Brand's free arm. At this point, Brand had sunken neck-deep in the quicksand. Hector was yelling for him to grab the hook, but there seemed to be a problem.

To get the hook Brand would have to let go of the sword. That was an unacceptable option as it might sink into the quicksand mix and never be found again. He felt like he was being tested to see if his commitment to the weapon was as strong as the weapon's powers. He would not let go, period.

As this was going on in his head Bubba and Hector could not understand why Brand was not grabbing the hook. They could see he had a weapon in hand, but all he had to do was drop the weapon and grab the hook.

Hector shouted down, "Bro, grab the hook!"

Brand needed to come up with some reason to not grab the hook, so he said "Need five minutes; too tired!"

What Brand could not see was the argument that began above the trap. Hector and Bubba were fighting on who would go down to help him. The fight did not last long because less than 90 seconds later, Hector was coming down to help.

At this point, Brand still had one arm above his shoulder with the mini sword in that hand but was chin high in quick-sand. Hector had the chain which was connected around one of his wrists. He came right down in front of Brand and, with a bear hug, wrapped the chain around him and gave Bubba a shout to start the winch.

Coming out of the trap was like being reborn. Rising from the grave. You can never appreciate life until you are looking at your imminent death. The air smelled like perfume, and the sky a magical blue with grass greener than ever seen before.

The realization of what just had occurred had not really sunken in for them. They had removed a monster from the world. A thing that had killed more people than anyone could know. Gabriel Hand was no more, and the world was a lot better because of it.

Bolt was aware that the knife was no ordinary knife. Even he did not have clearance to read the report concerning the creature called the Chameleon.

He was aware of certain aspects through indirect sources. The origin of the Chameleon is unknown, it may be from another galaxy or universe or a different plane of existence. What is known is that it can assume any shape, size, or color it desires. Also, it is alive and only bonds with one person at a time. They communicated telepathically, and once bonded, it is for the life of that person.

If that was not enough, the Chameleon could also adjust time, typically slowing it down relative to our time. Also, why Chameleon always picks a human companion is not known. Currently, it is undetermined how it makes that choice. It is believed it desires conversation periodically.

Bolt's instinct told him that after the event in the pit, Chameleon had chosen Subject 9.

Chapter 18

EQUILIBRIUM

Bubba and Hector were in the front seats of Bubba's truck while Brand laid in the bed. There is a special joy in knowing you have had a great day. That today you truly made a difference for the betterment of the world you live in. It brings a peacefulness that takes total control bringing waves of pleasure and joy within one's heart.

Brand was just basking in that field of joy.

As he lay in the back of the truck, he had a long conversation with his new friend. As they discussed many things, it seemed like hours to Brand, although the ride back to his rig was only 30 minutes away. By the end of their talk, they had established rules for communication. Which consisted of a ringing sound like a phone call within Brand's head, meaning Chameleon wanted to talk. And if Brand thought the words "Knock Knock" like he was in front of a door within his head, Chameleon would know he wanted to talk. If either responded mentally, not now, then there would be no conversation.

Chameleon explained that he could stop listening to all Brand's thoughts except for the word "Knock Knock" so he would have privacy. Chameleon also explained how it enjoyed being alone but sometimes wanted company in thoughts.

There was one last arrangement made; Chameleon became a tattoo on Brand's right arm. It was on the underside of the arm, with the sword's point starting just before his palm and traveling back to his elbow. There the handle started and worked its way to just before his armpit. It was a beautiful tattoo which seemed to never lose it's colors, having a 3D appearance and never looking totally flat.

When Brand did arrive home, little did he know one of his greatest joys would be taken away.

His thoughts were all over the board. One moment he was thinking about Amy. She is such a free spirit and makes him feel so young when she is around. He did miss her more than he thought proper.

He thought of how close to death he was and how, again there was no fear in its bite.

Once Gabriel was destroyed and Bubba saved, it would have been a fine death. No warrior could have asked for more. Then thoughts to his new friend Chameleon and how strange and wonderful a creature it is. His thoughts went to his first wife, who, even after 30 years apart, he still missed and wished he had been a better husband. Thoughts went to Hector and Bubba, who had just saved him from death's certainty. For such a short ride, he contemplated more than a man has any right to do.

It's amazing how there always seems to be a balance in life, in all things. Brand did not realize until he arrived back home and checked his iPhone that his very close friend Perry had died. She had four minor strokes and was recovering but today had one massive stroke that robbed the world of her forever.

She loved her mermaids and had collected all different forms, from pens with mermaid bodies to coffee cups. When she walked into the room, the air became magical.

Perry had helped Brand when he was at his lowest. She gave him shoes and shirts from her dead husband, barely knowing him at the time. More than that, she gave him her love which was shown with her time and care for his well-being. She provided that with no thoughts of reward or enrichment. Caring and giving simple out of love for another human being.

With three children and two grandchildren plus a brother and sister, she was the center that held it all together.

Brand could tell her everything with no reservations. She was totally non-judgmental plus honest with her own thoughts. They had wonderful Chinese buffet lunches and conversations. Thinking he would never have the joy of her company robbed him of his current happiness.

She could never be replaced. Even if Brand was 23, he would never find another Perry. He would never have those wonderful conversations and eat seafood with his best friend Perry again.

And that's the irony. On the one hand, Brand had killed Gabriel Hand. Someone extremely evil who deserved to die. On the other hand, Perry, his only mermaid, died too. Someone who had been good and kind. It was as if the universe was saying if someone really bad dies, then someone really good must also follow.

That balance, like the double edge sword, never stops. Always trying to kept some hidden equilibrium.

It was his best and worst day. Feeling great pleasure and pain but knowing the pleasure will fade far quicker than the pain. That type of pain lasts forever.

Part 3

Chapter 19

THE NOTE

It is said that the biggest mystery is one's own mind. With its curving corridors and hidden passages of areas never explored. Who can say they truly understand themselves

Brand liked to analyze himself as much as others. Always trying to understand why people do what they do, especially when just responding to impulse. So, the thought of having a road trip with Bubba was appealing. The plan was for them to go to Glenwood, NM, and take ownership of a DeLorean car.

Bubba, a big southerner, would drive the car back, and Brand would drive Bubba's truck. Of course, he could just have it transported here, but Bubba was not having it.

"This car is dear to my heart. I will drive my baby home," is how Brand remembered Bubba putting it. It did not hurt that Bubba was paying Brand well, and Brand being on Social Security, could always use the extra money.

Hector had found a nice woman. He had also become a Realtor. He was doing quite well at it. His bilingual abilities were helping him greatly in that field. Brand had always wished he could speak a second language.

There is a certain unspoken admiration to the people that can from the people that can't.

Hector's English was also much better than Brand had known. Brand had overheard him on the phone, and Hector was speaking perfect English. Most of the slang he used when around Brand was just show.

It did not surprise Brand at how well Hector was now doing. A good woman can really enhance capabilities that are already there but not being challenged. Hector was unavailable as he was closing two deals the week Bubba wanted to go.

Brand thought about what Hector had said. Bad things happen to people Brand does not like. Hector had left out that good things happen to people that Brand did like. In reality, it was much bigger than that, affecting businesses and countries.

But the thing getting to Brand was that whatever effect he had on others, it was impotent in regards to him.

Brand had been a realtor for over a year and had never sold a home. Even when he had been an Uber driver and had been passing out hundreds of business cards, not a single sale. It was definitely not because he did not want success or strive for it.

He was happy for Hector being a successful Realtor. It had the daily variety Brand had wanted while more or less being your own boss.

Brand's Sweetbull, or to the public just another pit bull, was already looking sad and not wanting the generous treats supplied to her.

Sweetbull and Brand had a truly special one-on-one connection. After years of just really having each other, sharing all foods excepts those that were harmful to dogs, and sleeping always together, Sweetbull was not happy!

Brand had talked to Roy, who gladly said he would take good care of her. Roy was an honest man which is hard to find these days. Very few would be trusted with Brand's girl, but Roy was one of the few.

Before Bubba and Brand were to leave, Brand had one request. He wanted them both to go to the bar ROCKY for a good luck meal. It had become a tradition, and the older Brand became, the more "traditions" there seemed to be.

For Bubba, it reminded him of when they had first met and how far things had changed.

Now they were the best of friends, and he said, "And you want the table in the back," with a big smile.

The bar ROCKY was an anomaly. It could easily be described as who it was not for. But the reverse is hard to say. Brand liked it because of its owner and the fact that it was never crowded. It always had that right mix of people.

It was dark and relatively small, but sounds within always seemed loud. None of the pictures on the walls had names attached, and everything looked old and well used, to be polite.

Yet there was a mix of people like Brand. They were hard to peg to this or that group. It seemed everyone had their own favorite spot.

Brand's seat was in the back in a recessed area where you get almost total privacy. Just as expected, it was open, and Bubba and Brand headed straight towards it. Just like the first time they met, Brand sat in the recessed back, which provides no view of anyone in the bar except at that table. Bubba sat on the opposite side of the recessed wall, facing Brand.

Joey, the owner, was there, and after Brand and Bubba got settled in and placed their order of foods and drinks, Joey came walking over.

Joey did not really do the work of the bar but was the best of bosses to work for. The crew he had seemed never to change and always were protective of him. That is because to be a friend of Joey was special. As great as he was to his friends, he could be stone cold when needed. He made all the decisions, and that was fine to his staff and customers.

Brand remembered the trust he had in those that lead him.

When you trust your commanding officer, you don't question. You just know your best interests are being served. Especially when in the spy business, you rarely know the big picture.

Joey was not large, being only 5 foot 6 inches with curly hair that was short, but he had a style that was impressive. He ignored Bubba as he definitely was not a regular but made a big deal of saying hello to Brand.

Joey started, "Man, it's been too long since I've seen you. Where you been hiding?" That was said with a big outstretched hand, looking for a handshake, which was returned by Brand.

Then Brand replied, "They only let me out for good behavior, and you know how I am," with a returned smile.

After the greeting, Bubba and Brand talked while waiting for the food. All seemed perfectly natural, but that is not what had happened.

During the handshake between Joey and Brand, Joey had secretly passed a note into Brand's hand. It was a small note with two sentences. Wrapped very tightly with a little sticky paste on the outside so when shaking someone's hand, it sticks firmly in the recipient's palm.

No electronics, just an old-fashioned hand-printed note which, by today's standards, is one of the most private means of communication. Brand had received it and then pocketed it with no one knowing, except Joey.

When things like that happen in the spy business, it is important to be patient. As much as Brand would have liked to have read it, knowing how he received it meant that it would have to be viewed in a very secure place. Meaning that all his known places were no good.

After the meal, they loaded into Bubba's truck. Bubba was eager to get his "baby." As they were working their way to the interstate, Brand suddenly announced that he was feeling really sick and to stop at the gas station to fill up the truck with gas while he used the restroom.

Bubba's truck had almost a full tank and did not need gas, but he had learned that Brand usually had a reason for things and trusting his friend complied.

When you think you're being watched, then everything you do has to be done in the public with a reason for what is seen. For example, when Joey passed the note to Brand, to the public, he was just saying hello. That was how the spy business used to be done. Everything in public with no one seeing anything.

Brand's curiosity was getting the best of him, and he had to read the note but in a private place. Preferably a place he had never been in. He also had to have a reason to get to that place so that if someone was watching him, it would look natural.

As Bubba started the process of filling the almost full tank, Brand went into the store to use the restroom. It had a typical men's bathroom with one private station at the back. Even though his feet could be seen, the rest of him was hidden. He retrieved the note, which was tightly folded within his pocket. After revealing the message, which consisted of two lines, no more than nine words, he used his lighter and burned it. Dropping what was left into the toilet then flushed the remains away.

It was serious. It would have to be addressed as soon as he returned from his road trip with Bubba. Brand was troubled and in deep thought but did not show it.

Lieutenant Colonel Bolt was feeling good in general. The last incident with Subject 9 turned out better than he could have imagined. Like a fine-tuned engine, all his agents were working perfectly, making it all look easy.

Bolt remembered his father talking about the football players of his time, "All the great players make it look easy." That was as true on the game field as in the intelligence agency.

Any good gambler will tell you knowing when to leave the game is just as important as knowing how to win.

Bolt did not like this road trip Bubba and Subject 9 were taking, but because they were monitoring with a more or less hands-off approach, he would have to deal with it. Deep down,

Bolt hated to feel out of control, and unknown to him, he had good reasons for that feeling.

They had decided to take two-hour shifts on the driving. Or, more precisely, Brand would drive no longer than two hours, so it was settled. The thing about long drives is it allows you to think about the past, present, and future without distraction.

The plan was to drive through the first night and day then get lodging for a good night's rest afterward. They really didn't take turns every two hours cause Bubba liked long drives, but Brand did drive a little.

Watching the world pass by through the windows reminded Brand of traveling through life. How some views stay the same for a time while other displays were random and brief.

The note Joey had given him came back to his mind, but he pushed it away again. He would have to deal with it, but this trip now with Bubba was like a vacation, and he just wanted to enjoy it.

As they settled into the trip and the time started to stretch, Brand asked Bubba if he thought this world was made for him?

Bubba responded with, "Heck, Yea. I have a home, trucks, and plenty of food, money, and my special girl."

Brand then said, "But why does outer space need to be so big? Why does the temperature change so drastically? Why is food so hard to get? It must be killed or grown, not to even mention that shelter has to be created."

Brand continued, "Imagine a barnacle attached to a ship. To him, the world is just perfectly made for him. He travels around the world on this structure made for him. After a time, he has friends there too, and they have a wonderful time together."

"But the truth is the ship was not built for them, and it travels around for its own purposes. The ship has no regard for the barnacles well being. When there becomes too many attached to the ship, they are removed."

What Brand was really asking is maybe in the big picture, none of this was really made for us. Maybe the true function of the universe has nothing to do with our well being.

To Brand, illusion, and reality were always getting confused. Most people kept their reality small, so there is no confusion. But when you start to expand your view of what might really be happening, reality starts to melt away, or more precisely, the illusion of reality disappeared, and the new reality begins.

For example, Bubba, Hector, and Brand had fought a demon and vampire that are not supposed to exist. But they do and now either have to be incorporated into this reality or denied to keep the current illusion going.

After their talk, both settled into the long drive ahead. Brand was thinking about the loss of Perry. His dear young friend, who at 45, left this world but will never leave his heart or be replaced. She was a light to her family and all those around her. Brand had cried at her funeral, and the pain was still fresh.

Bubba was thinking of his new acquisition, his "Baby," and life is made of those special moments. Each were lost in thoughts of their own, and the scenes beyond their windows changed as the people within our lives do.

Sometimes the hand of fate brings elements together that are a one in a million chance. Maybe it is not fate but some higher-order playing its hand or setting its mousetrap. Either way, there are times that a change in plans may save another's life, and it seemingly happens by chance.

Bubba and Brand were making excellent time and had stopped for a night's rest. When morning broke, they both felt rejuvenated. After a great sleep and food, with clear weather and good spirits, they were back on the road, with the destination either being one really hard day and night of driving or two much easier days. Of course, Bubba wanted the former as his baby needed him! Brand complied, knowing that feeling of getting close to something really special in one's life. It is a strong force, and he would not become an obstruction between Bubba and his DeLorean.

Chapter 20

CHANGE IN PLANS

Mary was a precocious child. At four years of life she understood much more than was ordinary for her age. Her parents were sad and worried about her brother, Thomas. Everyone called him Tommy. He was her older brother and now very sick. She saw her mother crying often and even her father when he was alone.

Tommy was two years older than Mary, being a happy normal boy until he started feeling sick. Then after many doctor trips, it was confirmed he had cancer. Mary could tell it was bad. This thing called cancer. That Tommy may die, and she worried that maybe she might get cancer too.

Her parents were taking Tommy to a special hospital that fixed just children. Mary liked the name of the hospital, which was called St. Jude Children's Hospital. Not only were they going to take Tommy to get well, but they also were going to stop at a big park for a family vacation.

Mary liked being outside and was eager to see the big park and have her brother feel better.

When they got there, she had never seen so much open space. She was at home in the wilderness. Having no fear and enjoying all the elements from the grass and flowers to the birds and even bugs. Her parents were taking extra care of Tommy, he had to use a wheelchair to get around, but she could tell he was en-

joying himself. That made her happy because she worried about him even at a young age.

Her parents thought that this may be the last family trip they all would have together. Tommy had a good time, and Mary seemed to love the park. But their time and attention were on Tommy. He was being so brave, and it all seemed so unfair.

They were traveling on a well-beaten path, Mary running about 10 feet ahead of the rest. There was so much to look at, and the scenario was so beautiful that the little bend in the path seemed like no threat at all.

There was one last fill-up of gas before they should have arrived at their destination. However, while at the gas station, there was a flurry of activity. After talking to some locals, Brand was informed that a little girl only four years of life was lost in the Gila National Forest. Her name was Mary and what Bubba and Brand had observed were some of the searchers getting ready for the search operation.

Edmund Burke had said, “The only thing necessary for the triumph of evil is for good men to do nothing.” As true today as when it was said over 200 years ago.

Usually, between Brand, Hector, and Bubba, they would come to some agreement over plans being taken. Typically, Brand would get his way, but each had conceded to the other at some time within their relationships.

Now Brand and Bubba were at an impasse. Bubba wanted to retrieve his DeLorean car, and Brand demanding that he was joining the search.

Brand saying, “Bubba, I understand but get an Uber and get your baby. I’ll drive your truck back as soon as she is found.”

Even though Bubba had never been in the military, he showed signs of being a great soldier. As much as you want to take it safe, you never leave your brothers in danger, especially in unknown territory.

Brand would not relinquish, and it was either he goes on his own or Bubba could accompany him.

Together in Bubba's truck, they followed the search parties into the forest.

There is a difference between wanting to win the lottery and wanting to save a life. The former is greatly desired but not expected. In the latter, a positive outcome is all that matters!

Bubba always had his trucks stocked well with supplies. Flashlights, plenty of water plus water filters, ropes, duct tape, guns, hunting knives, blankets, and MREs, also known as meals ready to eat. In addition, there was a tent and sleeping bags. Not only did he have all this, but it was already in two backpacks, ready to go. Say what you will, Bubba was always prepared and had the money to do things right.

It reminded Brand of an English philosophy on when to bring an umbrella. The answer is always as you never really know how the weather might be. Always better to have and not use than not have and need. The truth was because of Bubba being prepared, they were more than ready to help in the search.

Jack, the Park Ranger in charge, seemed less than happy to see Bubba and Brand following the search team to the command center. They were obviously not part of that group, but some feeling said let them help in the search, or maybe it was because Jack had a three-year-old at home. He allowed their help.

They arrived at an area that had a large makeshift shade covering with a large table and chairs. There was communication equipment within it. On the table was a large topography map showing the area in extreme detail.

Mary was only four years old and had been missing for seven hours. The search circle radius was 3 miles. This was assuming the age and landscape would make it almost impossible for her to have gotten further than that point, especially within the time she had been missing.

Bubba was at the back of the group inspecting the map, but Brand was right there in the front. Brand seemed to be studying the layout of the map, trying to imagine which way would be most favorable to a four-year-old.

When the group of searchers and the few park rangers were getting ready to begin the search, Brand found Bubba and stated there has been a change of plans.

"Bubba, I think Mary is on the other side of the valley, past the three-mile radius search area." Bubba was just standing there and had no reply.

Brand continued, "I have been studying the map, and we need to drive to the other side of this valley and search from there moving towards here."

Park Ranger Jack was not surprised when he saw the two misfits who were trying to be part of the searchers leave the area. In a way, he was happy. He felt that they would only bring trouble. Searches are hard and really should only be done by experienced, trained personnel.

Poor Mary's parents, as if they did not have enough problems. Between all the worrying they have been going through with Tommy. Now the guilt of losing their only daughter in a huge national park.

Bubba was mad but knew there was no point arguing, so they boarded his truck and started the journey to the other side of the valley. They had been up for over 14 hours, but each had adrenaline pumping for different reasons. Neither was tired.

During the ride, which was relatively short, no words were exchanged. Bubba was not happy and just wanted to pick up his DeLorean. He was driving fast while Brand seemed to be in a trance. When they arrived, wherever that was, it was known by Brand saying, "Stop right here!"

Chapter 21

BRAND IS MISSING

Gila National Forest has over three million acres comprising of forests, hills, and rugged mountains with deep canyons and rangeland. It's best known for its wilderness areas and was established in 1924 as the first designated wilderness reservation by the US Government.

To people who spend time in nature's home, this beautiful untouched landscape can not be described to any who have not seen it.

If you're religious, you can see God's hand in its design. The national parks and forests remind us to be humble and how great Earth's beauty really is.

The view Brand and Bubba had was beautiful, with trees everywhere rising up to the top of the valley's ridge. The colors looked like they were just painted on each area seen. There were beautiful shades of greens, blues, and browns. The flowers of yellow and purple scattered about like freckles, creating a picture that looked like it was painted by a master artist.

They started to walk their way from the truck parked on the side of the roadway into the woods leading to the slope before the ridge. It was a hard walk, and the backpacks made it none the easier. Brand's spirits were high, and it was like he knew he would find Mary but time was still of the essence.

Bubba, being the stronger of the two men and mad with adrenaline, was leading the way, with Brand following in the quake.

They would only have about four hours before it would get dark, and Bubba had no intentions of being there that long. His thoughts were on being so close to his prize and having Brand torpedo it without a thought to his regard. Deep down, he believed they had no chance of finding this child, Mary, and were just wasting time.

As Bubba turned around to address the amount of light left.

Either they would have to turn around in two hours or walk back in the dark. The worst-case scenario was stay the night.

Something was wrong.

There were absolutely no sounds around him. No birds, insects, running water, or even a leaf in the wind. Nothing.

Also, Brand was nowhere to be seen. So within seconds Bubba was shouting part out of anger and part out of concern for his friend, "BRAND! BRAND! BUDDY! WHERE YOU AT?" Absolutely nothing. It was like Bubba had just landed in a place with no life or sounds. There was not even a slight breeze.

As Brand was following Bubba, suddenly there was electricity in the air. Looking to his right, he could see what appeared a path barely used but definitely different from what lay on either side. The thought of Bubba was far from Brand's mind.

A certainty in his head said, follow this to find Mary. Without hesitation, Brand had started walking it.

After a few steps, the world seemed to be changing again. Now there was a mist that came from nowhere and was everywhere. As he noticed it, it became thicker and all-encompassing. Then the path he was walking became wider and more defined, opening up to a circular clearing 30 feet wide surrounded by trees.

At this point, Brand felt that place was holy, and he removed his shoes and socks, placing each sock within a shoe and aligning the shoes neatly together. When his feet touched the grass within the circle of trees, it was wonderful. It was a feeling like just having gotten out of a shower with the temperature at a perfect balance of not hot or cold but perfect and clean. A peace that flooded the body and spirit.

Then as if that were not enough, he saw his first wife standing there, smiling at him. She had such a beautiful smile, and he still was so in love with her.

At one of the corners of his mind, he knew that all this was impossible. He had loved her with all his heart but showed it in the dumbest of ways. If he could redo it, have a second chance to make it right. Brand could not resist going to the vision of his first wife.

If Bubba was mad before, he was really upset now. This time though, it was with himself. Funny how the mind thinks. For as he was now in panic mode, he remembered a TV show Brand loves, *Doctor Who*. They all had watched it together one day, and afterward, Hector and Bubba agreed. They were the companions, and Brand was the Doctor. The job of the companions was to keep the Doctor alive.

Bubba's thoughts went to how could he have lost Brand? It was his job to keep him okay. He should have been walking in front of me so I could have kept an eye on him. How can I go back home and face Hector, Roy, and worst yet, Sweetbull without Brand?

Men in war know that feeling. One moment your comrades are fine, and the next, you're taking a long walk home without them. It's a long hard walk, and the feeling of loss is overwhelming.

Bubba just couldn't move. He knew he should contact the park ranger, but if Brand were to just re-appear and Bubba was not there, that also would be bad.

Now the DeLorean meant nothing to him. He would be happy just to return home with his friend. He also thought about what Brand had asked him, if the world was made for him. How his answer now would be different. Now he would like to know always where his friends were and if they were in trouble. Now Bubba was starting to understand what Brand was asking.

"How could we lose internal and external tracking? I thought that technology could be located anywhere on the planet?" Lieutenant Colonel Bolt was quite upset and the answers he was receiving only increased his aggravation.

Bolt continued, and the tone in his voice was make it happen yesterday, "Get Army Rangers plus Indian trackers and heat choppers on it now. I want him found. Use the cover story that you are looking for the child that went missing. Contact me when the package is found!"

Park Ranger Jack just knew it was going to be a bad day, and it was only getting worse. Now he was dealing with FBI Special Agent Rod, and she was all business. Jack started to say, "I will not use any of my team to search for a grown man while we still have a missing four-year-old out there."

Tanisha Rod actually was a special agent, so her FBI title of Special Agent Rod was very appropriate. She was top of her class and always pushed harder than what was needed. Tanisha had pride in closing cases, hopefully, closed in a positive way, but bottom line, an answer is found, and the case is resolved. She believed in what she could see, never in supernatural or paranormal answers.

The facts were two men went into the woods, and only one came back. The other is either in the woods or playing a trick on his friend. If we assume it is the former, then we will find him or at least find something. Special Agent Rod knew this was important because getting Army Rangers involved in something like this is unheard of. To also have Indian trackers plus Rangers meant they really wanted this man found or at least answers as to what occurred.

She looked at Park Ranger Jack, saying, "I have no intentions of using your men for our search. It will be conducted on the other side of the valley. Keep your people on your side, understand?"

Then she continued, "If you find either the child or man, then contact us as we will also do the same if either is found."

Jack was surprised as he expected her to take over the search for Mary, but she was more concerned about him invading her area. To Jack, that was fine because a four-year-old could never get that far. But he really wanted whatever help she had, helping him find Mary!

Bubba had not left the area that Brand disappeared from, hoping that he would reappear and all would be fine. But as seconds turned to minutes which led to hours, his hopes faded, and sadness began to take over. Bubba knew that if anyone could just reappear, it would be Brand, and he knew Brand would not leave if the situation was reversed. So, he tried to keep his hopes high and man his station until Brand came back.

When Special Agent Rod encountered Bubba, the Choppers had already started their search. The Army Rangers and Indian trackers had also started searching seemingly ignoring Bubba. For his part, Bubba was just turning slightly in circles staying approximately in the same area, more in shock than any help or threat.

Special Agent Rod started with, "Sir, I need you to tell me exactly what happened and leave no detail out!" It was said with authority. Disobeying was not an option.

Bubba babbled his story out. There really was not much to tell or many details to share. The displeasure was clear on Rod's face when she said, "Thank you. You can go now."

Sometimes in a fight, there is a punch or a sound, something that wakes you up. It has been called a second wind or an adrenaline rush, but with it, you have no fear and all the energy needed to finish whatever is at hand.

Bubba had just woken up!

"NO, I will NOT leave my friend lost in this forest!"

Bolt had been monitoring Bubba via the audio on his phone since Subject 9 became missing. Bolt also was on the speaker with special agent Rod's boss.

Bolt commanded, "Tell her to let him stay!" As his words were spoken within seconds, Rod's boss was saying in her two-way communications, "Let him stay for now." With that, the tension was defused, Bubba was staying. Special agent Rod was now putting all her attention into the search, and Bolt was feeling good. He may have lost Subject 9, but at least he still was in control. Mistakes happen but retaining power was always the end game.

As soon as the drama between Bubba and Special Agent Rod was settled within minutes, a nasty storm came rolling into the area. After one hour, all searches had to be canceled because of the dangerous wind speeds and a torrential downpour of rain providing zero visibility.

Chapter 22

SHIP OF ALIENS

Brand was moving to the center of the circle, going to meet the vision of his first ex-wife, but before he arrived at his destination, he blacked out.

When Brand regained consciousness, it was like his mind was flooded with knowledge. Not just thoughts but also seeing images with detailed information all in his mind. Then the thoughts became sounds which turned into words. But more than that for each word seemed to have feelings attached. This was more than an inflection of sound but feeling the word's meaning within his body.

He knew he was on a ship, and the ship was not on Earth. It was not a guess. He just knew it was right. Now his mind was talking to him. Answering his own questions with facts.

Brand also had a feeling that time moved differently where he was. It moved slower relative to Earth. This being only a feeling, but it created a sense of urgency.

He remembered a story about a man in a hole, well over the reach of his arms. He was stuck in the hole until a snake was thrown in. It's amazing what urgency can do.

At that same moment, it seemed like a wall disappeared, for now, he was in a room full of aliens. Brand did not remember moving. It was like they all were now in the room with him.

Also, he noticed that the light was everywhere and originated from nowhere. It was odd, as there were no shadows. Another oddity was that he was taking all this in but not feeling scared or shocked as he imagined he would feel in this type of situation.

His thoughts had now come back to his reality which was that Mary was on this ship, and they needed to get back to Earth very quickly, considering the time factor.

There were at least four different alien creatures in front of him. Here is a brief description of each creature and then what they were arguing about.

There was an insect-like organism, but it was huge compared to the ones on earth. It was about the size of a six-foot man. It looked similar to a praying mantis. It was wearing a cape-like jacket that started under the face and went to the top of its legs. You could feel it was very smart and in charge.

The praying mantis had four little grey aliens by it. Each of the little grey aliens looked very similar. Their skin had a smooth look to it, being greyish. Their heads were large compared to their three-and-a-half feet height. They had large black eyes that resembled a cat's eyes but started more on the side of their heads and finished around the front. No ears that were apparent and a slit for a month and two small openings for a nose in the general spot where a nose should reside.

There was also one large greyish blue alien that was on the praying mantis' side, It's skin had an elephant texture and was grey but had blue patches forming lines making him look like little rivers were pasted on him. His black eyes were large but more round than the little grey aliens. His month also was more defined than the little greys. He had a nose that was small and protruding high cheekbones. He looked different than the two large greys opposing them.

On the other side, the two large greys had a slightly pinkish color grey with no blue color tones or highlights. Their skin was also smoother looking than the one on the praying mantis side. Their faces looked less defined because their mouth and nose were smaller than the large grey they were facing.

The two large greys also had a dragon-like creature that was at least nine feet tall with scales and a large tail. The color of the scales started as a light brown but turned to gold past the midpoint of its frame. Its body resembling strength and power, yet there was also a sense of old age and wisdom to the creature. It's malevolent nature, even though not shown, was well apparent to everyone around it.

Brand seemed to understand the entire conflict even though no words were spoken. His extra senses seemed to have been opened like when a blind person has been given sight. It was amazing and cannot truly be appreciated unless felt.

The praying mantis and Brand were in direct contact with each other.

Brand said within his mind, "Mary and I need to get back to Earth quickly."

The response in his mind from the praying mantis was, "It will be done." This was sent into his mind, but the word's feelings were comforting to his body and spirit.

Then the trouble began with one of the greys. There were two, but one had a two-inch gold pendant that wrapped around the neck and came together at the chest. The other grey who was in charge was irate and demanding the container be transferred as he had already paid for it.

Brand seemed to know certain things without being told anything. He knew the gold pendant was a weapon and that grey was a bodyguard to the grey demanding the container. The container was a reference to Mary as Brand knew the large grey wanted to use her body for its time at Earth. Brand could also tell this was a very important being, as before, the thoughts had feelings attached to them, so he could feel the grey's ego was huge.

The Praying Mantis did not seem moved or troubled in the least and said without any words, "He is one of the chosen, and the Council of Nine has stated that all chosen's wishes will be honored. He wishes to take the container and go back to Earth. So, it will be done." That was sent without emotion purely as a matter of fact, or at least that was the way the thoughts felt to Brand that he received.

With that, there was shouting by the large Grey wanting Mary as its container. The shouting, which was not shouting but thoughts, did not just hurt one's ears but made Brand's whole body hurt. Like wanting to throw up and having a fever with a bellyache all at the same moment. It was intense and conveyed the anger that was felt.

During this time, his bodyguard had his hand close to where the two sides of the pendant meet, which Brand knew was the trigger to the weapon.

The Praying Mantis conveyed that it had already been decided, and the two greys and the Dragon man should depart. Other arrangements for them will be provided.

This just seemed to make matters worse as the large grey became even more upset. He stated that this was not over and that he could easily destroy this ship plus much of Earth if he desired. Release the container to his possession, or a war with the Reptoids, which was the Dragon man, and his group may become inevitable. He wanted an immediate hearing to resolve the matter.

The tension in the room had become heavier, making even breathing a more laborious task. It was like pressure within the room was sitting upon one's chest and mind. Even thinking was more difficult.

It seemed to affect everyone in the room except the Praying Mantis. The small greys had begun to form a wide half-circle around the Praying Mantis, with the good large grey seemingly transmitting a request for help.

The Praying Mantis projected that this *was* the intervention. All was foreseen by the Council of Nine. That is why they collected the container so it can be returned. Other arrangements have been made for their regards.

Now the angry grey tried to reason with the Praying Mantis projecting that Brand is the lowest form of life. Why should anyone, especially himself, bow to its wishes? That Brand could hardly hear or speak and should not be allowed to make any decision, let alone something that involves its business.

Again, the answer was Brand was one of the chosen, and all chosen wishes were to be honored by the proclamation of the Nine. The discussion is over, and the angry grey's actions will be watched. There shall be no retribution to Brand or Mary, or war will start!

At this point, Brand was surprised. How could someone as unimportant as himself or Mary matter that much? How could their well-being or lack of it start a war?

It reminded him of being in the woods and having no worries or problems. All that is needed is a bear that has your back.

There are so many levels to all things, with each level affecting others. Some are connected, and others where no connection is apparent.

Brand and Mary were seemingly unimportant, and yet that just was not the case. Forces they knew nothing about were ready to start a war on their behalf. Brand's thoughts went to how much of life is like that? Where forces unseen affect us for good or bad in such drastic ways.

Then things changed again, like pressure being released, the tension eased, and a resolution had been established. Now Brand heard the details of their return. Mary would be implanted with false memories of a nice bear that provided care for her.

Unknown to Brand, he had been picked up before and left with either false or no memories of the events. This time it was to be different. It was decided he would retain all memories of this time, for it was now the proper time for his awakening.

Chapter 23

LOST AND FOUND

After the downpour of rain and two more days of searching, the mood was low and sour. They had found nothing. The dogs were useless, especially after the rain. The choppers had found no significant heat signatures. Neither Special Agent Rod's Army Rangers and Indian trackers nor Park Ranger Jack's searchers had found anything. Not even clothes or tracks. It was like they had just vanished. As a rock dropped into a pond making no ripples, just disappearing under the water forever.

Then it happened. Brand's shoes were found. They were perfectly dry and found exactly together, both pointing in the same direction with each sock placed inside each shoe.

Like a light at the end of the tunnel, hope was renewed. All resources were used at the same time, feeling like they still had a chance of at least a recovery.

Special Agent Tanisha Rod had almost lost hope. She was thinking this case will halt or at least haunt her career. She could not understand how nothing could be found. There is always evidence left, no matter how small to locate. So, with the advent of Brand's shoes being found, it was something.

Of course, now new questions needed answers. That area was searched many times before finding the shoes. They were in good condition, seemingly unaffected by the storm. Who had put them there and why? Special Agent Rod liked answers, and this case was only bringing more questions.

As Mary and Brand were walking back to the main path, just before they were found, Mary looked at Brand and said, "I know you will fix my brother!" Then she gave him a little hug and proceeded walking. Brand said nothing, thinking how hard this ordeal must be on her young mind.

It was not until the next day that Mary and Brand were found. They were together. Given that they were missing for four days, they were in remarkably good shape. Both were dehydrated, but no apparent bruises were seen.

Mary had no idea how long she had been gone or where she had been. All that she remembered was just that a nice bear made her feel safe, and then she saw Brand.

Brand remembered the entire event and how it only seemed like two or three hours but turned into four Earth days. He was not going to tell them what he saw and understood had happened.

First, they would never believe him, and worst, Bakers Act him. Which in Florida means they take you away for at least three days of observations. Brand knew he was not crazy and was not imagining what he had experienced.

After the confrontation with the aliens, the two greys and the Draconian left angry, saying that this was not over, as it was over. Then Mary and Brand were teleported back to the area of the circle in the clearing, about half-mile away. This occurred through a beam of light that first filled the room they were in. Then this light which was a bluish-purple, seemed to intermingle with their bodies. Once that occurred, the floor's bottom disappeared with the light, Mary and Brand racing to the spot where they were eventually found in. When they touch the ground, the light disappeared, and they were solid again.

Brand was not going, to tell the truth and instead said he got lost but found Mary on the third day and was working his way back when found. Asked why he removed his shoes and socks, he had no answers.

Park Ranger Jack was just happy they were found, as were most of the searchers and all involved.

Except for Special Agent Rod. She knew Brand was lying and definitely knew more than he was revealing about the event. There were many questions regarding this case that were not and probably would never be answered. It would look fine for her report, but it bothered her. She was a true professional and knew if the right questions were asked, it would reflect badly on her performance.

To say Bubba was happy surely would be an understatement. You would have thought he won the lottery or that Brand was his long-lost brother. He rushed up to Brand, thanking Jesus and hugging him as men will do when in war, thinking the other hadn't survived.

It was a few moments before Bubba's anger showed.

"Where the heck did you go?! Why did you not answer me?"

Brand knew he would tell Bubba and Hector the entire story but not now. He was happy to be on planet Earth again, smiling, thinking about all the things we take for granted.

Brand saw the moment Tommy realized Mary was okay. The love in his expression was truly heartwarming. The next instant, he started to understand Mary's statement about fixing Tommy, who was still in his wheelchair.

Mary's Mom had tears of joy running down her face as she expressed her thanks for looking and finding their precious Mary. When Brand asked about Tommy, she explained his condition and their plans on going to St. Jude Children's Hospital for a possible cure.

Even with finding Mary, Brand felt sad. He now so wished he could help Tommy and felt helpless in that regard.

Mary's parents' love for Brand that day was like a 50-year marriage squeezing all the most loving moments into 10 minutes. They hugged him, thanked him profusely, had taken pictures of him, him and Mary, and then the five of them together.

They wanted to take Brand to the hospital, but he would have none of that. Bubba, who had finally started to act like himself, also wanted to get out of there as quickly as possible.

Bubba started with, "I'll drive most of the way home. You just stay in eyesight."

Brand was just looking at him like he had lost his mind.

"Aren't you forgetting something? Your "Baby" Miss DeLorean," Brand said with a big smile.

Bubba had completely forgotten about his baby, which showed with his return grin.

"I have new plans for her." With that, he was on the phone making new arrangements, which consisted of raised voices from Bubba and the seller on the phone.

After that was settled and they were back in Bubba's truck, Brand had that look. It was hard to describe but always easy to tell when apparent.

"Bubba, I have a question," after a long pause, "Am I getting paid for the time I went missing?"

With that and a big smile and laugh, they were on their way home from a road trip gone bad and then good. Bubba had to pay more for the delay in taking ownership and extra costs in having it transported to Florida.

Brand, on the other hand, had a veil removed, and his paranormal abilities were not enhanced but allowed to operate freely. There was a whole range of abilities he now knew he had, and was eager to test his range in controlling them. The joy of bringing Mary back to her parents was priceless.

Lieutenant Colonel Bolt was listening to the report from his top agent, this time with no interruptions. The internal tracking devices are all nonoperational, but the external ones are working fine.

It is believed that while Subject 9 was missing, he was no longer on the planet, which lined up with all the facts at hand. The actual events were not verified, only assumed.

Bolt knew he was back in charge but was he really? He enjoyed being at the top and knowing most of the secrets that are hidden from all without a need to know.

His gut feelings were that he was being played. Even worse than not being in charge is thinking you are even when you are not. Bolt's instinct was shouting things have changed concerning Subject 9.

Illusion and reality are often confused. Take a broken heart that thought their lover's love was true. Or someone who seemed rich until they were found to be dirt poor.

There are so many examples that defy what we believe to be our reality but are excluded from the mind as a safety measure providing a sense of peace. But deep down in one's heart of hearts, the mysteries of this world greatly exceed the reality imagined.

Part 4

Chapter 24

JOEY IS UPSET

Living in Florida has pluses, especially when winter arrives. Even with the great weather, Brand was feeling his age in pains from all directions. It had been an action-packed year.

There was the haunted house and the vampire Gabriel Hand, not to mention the aliens and Mary at Gila National Forest. Now the note Joey had passed him had to be handled.

Before Brand's pain could be eased, his greatest pleasure had to be addressed. Sweetbull, his pit bull, always demanded attention in the morning. Living alone in his trailer, she was his light at the end of the tunnel.

Being that Brand went to bed after and arose before Sweetbull's slumber, he prepared himself and was ready when she jumped off the bed and started to yawn. She would give Brand the look like it's time for our walk. Who could deny those eyes? Definitely not Brand. So, a good walk and then the first of many treats to follow.

Hector and Bubba were stopping over for a cookout but really to find out what happened during Brand's disappearance. Even Bubba had no idea, and he had been there the entire time. So, they were both eager to hear the story Brand had to tell.

The banquet consisted of hot dogs and hamburgers with plenty of sauerkraut, onions, and bacon. The fixings also had ketchup and mustard with beers, soda, and water to finish the feast. They had watermelon for dessert, and after hearing the tale Brand had told, there was not a sound.

No matter how many new experiences one encounters in life that change our perspective, the next one is still a shock. Brand could see that on their faces even after all they had been through.

Before another sound could be heard or said, a car came screaming down the main road breaking its speed to make the 90-degree turn to enter the farm. The car stopped abruptly where the party of three were sitting. All were staring in silence.

Brand knew what was happening. The note had said, "I have a chance to get my son back." From most fathers, it would imply something good. Many fathers have a great love for their children, and gaining access to them really is a beautiful thing.

This was all wrong, though. Joey's son Bill had died tragically, but isn't every death tragic? Each person has great potential, and some take a long time before they shine. Bill was not coming back, and Joey did not have any chance in making that happen.

Brand had met Joey the day before the cookout. They went out on Joey's boat, of course leaving their phones at Joey's bar ROCKY. Even if they still were being monitored, it felt better knowing you made your opponent work for it.

Brand and Joey did undercover work for the Government back in their early years. Brand's role was just someone who came in, picked up information from the real spy, and then gets it back to whoever sent him out there.

Joey, on the other hand, was the real deal. It takes nerves to do what Joey did. Recording people who would kill you in a second if they even suspected you were an undercover agent trying to destroy them.

Who really knows what Joey did or was capable of doing? In that regard even the most normal person can astound you given non-normal circumstances.

Doing what Brand and Joey did involved not just having nerves like steel but being smart, real smart, and thinking fast on your feet.

So, when Brand told him to forget it, he was being played, the anger he received was genuine. Brand tried to persuade him with logic and then pleaded with him that nothing good can come from this.

A father's love cannot be measured, and Joey was a father like none other.

Joey almost drove into Brand's rig as he parked and exited the vehicle moving towards the group.

Joey's look at Brand had said, or more like commanded, "We need to talk."

Brand and Joey entered his 5th wheel, and that's when the shouting started. Some things could be heard rather clearly while other sounds were muffled inside Brand's home.

From Joey shouting, "IT WILL WORK!"

And Brand's response, "Joey, PLEASE, think about it. Even if it does it will never be right!" Then the voices were lower, but everyone could clearly hear Joey say, "I thought you would help me. NEVERMIND!"

The response could not be heard outside where Hector and Bubba were, but inside was said in a low voice, "Joey, I AM trying to help you! Please just do nothing and think about it more. PLEASE!"

Chapter 25

TREASURE HUNT

After Joey had left, which was just as fast as when he arrived, all were speechless. Then with a delayed silence that seemed to last two eternities, Brand said, "Joey's a bit upset," and that was it.

Then he changed the subject to what he was going to say just before Joey's explosion upon them.

"How about we go on a treasure hunt in the Gulf. I know a spot that might be lucky!" Well, it didn't take much prodding for all to agree.

Bubba would rent a boat and scuba gear for two as it was always safer to have someone remain on the boat when diving. Hector would take care of the food and drinks. Being that Brand knew the secret spot containing the loot, was his price of admission.

Most people who live in Florida are less than 15 minutes from the water. That water might be the Atlantic Ocean or the Gulf of Mexico. Either side is beautiful. In this case, it would be the Gulf of Mexico. The waters there are more mellow than the Atlantic and sometimes can be too warm. To scuba divers it is wonderful.

Scuba diving is like exploring a new and totally different world. It's more like exploring outer space than anything else on the planet's surface. For one thing, you can become perfectly balanced in water, giving you the ability to move in all directions. Also, the fact that you need oxygen and everything around you makes it feel like an alien environment, and you are the invader. Brand loved to dive and was really looking forward to tomorrow when it would occur.

Deep down or right on the top, it's hard to describe where the feeling came from, but what could not be denied was that it was strong and screaming big trouble was coming.

It was not a hard prediction, given that Joey would probably do the worst thing.

It was even bigger than that, something saying this is the biggest event that will happen in his life. Brand knew that if it turned out bad, it would be devastating, but to how many besides himself?

Lieutenant Colonel Bolt was in a rare mood. Not unhappy, which would be a rare event, but not paranoid either. He was having a content, almost numb feeling, which hindered his usual thinking. The monitor we all use to judge our actions are usually self-reflection without much outside stimulus, which works as long as our brain is processing correctly.

The day was beautiful, and for a Floridian to say that is really something. Of course, Brand would never be a Floridian no matter how long he lived in the state.

To be a real Floridian, you have to be born in Florida, period. But even without the title, the day was perfect.

Hector and Bubba were there to pick him up, and they had everything they needed for a successful adventure. Only Brand knew he was just following a feeling.

After the visit with the aliens, he was more aware of those feelings. This time it said to go to the water, there is a prize waiting for you. When he asked himself where, the reply was, you will know when you're there.

Once aboard the rented motorboat, which are readily available where they live, and after all the supplies were transferred from the truck to the 36-foot boat, with an inside cabin, the big questions were asked.

Hector was first to say, "Bro, where are we going, and how long is it going to take?"

Brand then gave Bubba that look like I told you so with a big grin on his face.

Brand answered, "Bubba tell Hector where and when, please."

Now it was Bubba who had a big smile saying, "Who knows?"

Which, of course, was right as Brand said, "I'll tell you when I know."

They headed out with Brand saying, now more to your right or make a 45-degree turn here or there. It seemed all very random, and then all of a sudden came the, "STOP," shouted from Brand. Now if you ask Brand, he never shouts, just talks loudly, but it halted all further motion as they were now in the middle of nowhere.

Everything changes when you go below the surface, as true with people as it is with the water. First, sound changes in that you can hear sounds or vibrations from quite a distance. Depending on the water and surface conditions it can be as clear as glass or like a mud storm.

Between the water pressure and the temperature changes, plus time and amount of oxygen consumed each dive is different. Even for two divers on the same day, there are a lot of variables.

On this day, Bubba and Brand were to dive because both were certified. That, of course, did not stop the argument before the dive on whether Bubba or Hector would accompany Brand for the treasure.

In the end, diving is not to be toyed with, and there are risks on any dive. The standard operating procedure is to always do the buddy system, meaning always dive with at least another person who is watching your back.

As they proceeded down into the waters of the Gulf, the world they knew became forgotten. Sure, there is plenty of beauty on top of the water, but ask anyone who dives, and they'll say it's a foreign world with dangers and beauty abundant.

Anything dropped over a boat or ship will end up on the water's bottom. Whether rings or other types of jewelry, there is always the chance of finding something valuable. With that said, just looking anywhere is like finding the proverbial needle in a haystack.

But on beautiful days like this, being underwater is always good. The view is worth everything, and they were not disappointed.

The way the buddy system is supposed to work is each diver keeps an eye and is within arm's reach of the other. Brand never believed in it. Diving was always a solo experience for him. Brand led the way, and with the events of him missing recently, Bubba was behind him on one side close enough to grab a leg if needed. Bubba was a strong man, and it was easy to keep up with Brand.

It seemed like Brand was swimming under the water the same way he had given directions on the boat. A random turn here and there with no clear direction or purpose that can be determined. But within ten minutes of reaching the bottom, which was only 70 feet deep, something seemed to wink.

There was a little hill on the water's bottom, and merged within the hill, something was giving off light intermittently. It was like a flash and then gone. If it wasn't for the flashing, Bubba would never have noticed it. Brand was swimming directly to it, and after a bit of wrestling it out of the sandy hill, the prize was his.

Brand had a diver's bag like he knew he would find something, or maybe it just good luck to bring on any dive. Today the possession found went quickly into the bag, which was securely attached to Brand. Then he gave Bubba a hand sign of let's go back to the boat and inspect what had just been found.

Usually, Brand hates to leave any air in his air tank as the joy of being under the water deserves all the time he has, meaning an empty air tank when done. But today was different, and inspecting the newly acquired object was all that mattered.

The thrill of diving is you never know what you may find or encounter. Most of the time, it is a wonderful feeling but sometimes can be fearful. They were traveling back to the boat with Brand leading the way and Bubba close to his left foot's fin.

Besides alligators and vicious ants, Florida also has its share of sharks. Most of the time, sharks, when you're underwater, don't bother you. It's when your splashing on the surface that they become aggressive. Of course, this is just what usually happens. Each experience is unique.

Sharks have the normal five senses of a human plus two additional ones. They have the human senses of sight, touch, hearing, taste and smell. Their sense of smell is incredible, and a single drop of blood can attract their attention a quarter of a mile away, spelling a creature's doom. As if that was not enough, they also have an electromagnetism ability which makes them extremely aware of electric fields. And for good measure, they are also finely aware of water pressure.

Brand instantly stopped moving vertically and straighten to a horizontal position. While at the same time making a 180-degree turn, so he was now facing the direction he was traveling away from. The move was so sudden and performed so smoothly that Bubba had already swum past Brand before he realized Brand had stopped.

By the time Bubba turned and faced Brand, who now had turned again towards the direction of the boat, the men were face to face. The boat loomed about 30 feet from them, not counting the 60 feet to the surface.

Brand had unclipped his diver bag thrusting it to Bubba. Then he pointed to Bubba and forcefully pointed to the boat. He repeated this action twice, and Bubba knew he wanted him to go to the boat with their prize.

Bubba hated when Brand became forceful regarding something he wanted to do, but he knew in his heart that it always was for a good reason. But he still disliked it. Also after losing Brand during their last adventure, he would comply but still keep his eyes on Brand the entire time.

Bubba let some air into his vest so that he slowly was rising to the surface. He also was watching Brand who had turned back away from the boat and was just making a cross of himself in the water. He had his arms out from his sides with his legs together, just perfectly balanced and seemingly waiting.

Bubba was 10 feet from the surface with the boat about 20 feet from him, giving him a stadium view of Brand. This now provided a great area view and is when he first spotted the trouble.

There were 3 sharks with the largest being 14 feet and in the center. The other 2 were smaller and flanking the big shark on either side. The smaller ones were widening their distance from the center shark to be able to attack Brand from both sides at once.

Bubba first thought was that at the speed the sharks were moving he would never have enough time to go down there and help his friend. His second thought was how could Brand had known about the impending danger. He was swimming with his back towards it until he turned around.

Now Bubba's full attention was on Brand. He noticed that Brand had not even pulled out his knife. At the distance and speed the sharks were approaching, he surely must see the large one heading directly to him. There would be about three or four seconds until all three sharks would be upon him.

Brand now moved his arms in a circular motion until they were in front of him. Then with his palms towards his body moved them towards his stomach. Once there he made an invisible ball with his palms and then rapidly rotated his palms away from his body while also thrusting his arms in a 45-degree direction.

What happened next can only be explained that you had to be there to believe it. Bubba was watching and could see everything extremely clearly. The problem was what he was seeing was hard to describe and even harder to believe unless seen.

Right after Brand's movement with his arms, there was a flashing of light. It was like a strobe light effect but with little electrical charges that looked like they had physical properties with little pointers at the ends of each light ray. They were moving like lightning in all directions. Even more than that, it was not just in all directions but occupying all the space from the bottom of the gulf's floor to about 30 feet above. This effect surrounded Brand and extended 20 feet from him in all directions.

Once the effect permeated the three sharks they each turned and left the area immediately. Just as Bubba had felt that before the sharks were going to attach, he now felt like they had left the area for their own safety. The whole event lasted maybe two seconds and then Brand was swimming straight for the boat.

There are times you see something, but it is so strange that it just gets put in a dusty corner of the mind, to be examined and understood later. This was one of those cases. He would ask Brand about it but not now.

Brand quickly met Bubba, and they together met the boat.

It seemed like energy was in the air. Hector noticed instantly that Brand's diver bag was with Bubba and definitely had something inside, and as he helped Bubba back on board, he asked, "Bro, what you find?" And then, "What's with the flash of light down there?"

To the second question, Bubba knew the answer but was not going to go there. Brand had made no response to both questions.

The truth was, even Brand did not really inspect what he had put into the diver's bag once he found it. There was a strong impulse to get it back to the boat. In regards to the light event that had just happened he also had no answers, just questions.

Now in the cabin with the boat anchored, the time was right to reveal the answer to Hector's first question, what was found.

It was a crystal skull perfectly cut with a shape being 5 inches wide and 7 inches tall and 5 inches deep.

It was an amazing piece of art that instantly made one think of its history. Who carved it? When was it created? How did it find its way to the Gulf's watery bottom?

It could be sold, but even though Brand was tight on money, which was an always event, there was never a thought of selling it. As a matter of fact, Brand said he had the perfect spot in his trailer for it. He did want to find the value and come up with the money to pay Bubba and Hector their share of the profit.

That was agreed by all three men. Later Bubba told Brand privately he did not want any money as he already had plenty.

Brand could tell that Bubba really enjoyed the excitement of their adventures. Since Bubba had enough money and was not driven by the obsession of always wanting more, the trip was payment enough for him.

Hector was definitely gaining more possessions and money. He was on his way up the ladder. This seemed directly connected to the new woman in his life.

Brand was happy for him, but possessions and money can ruin the best of people. He was concerned for him even though, by all accounts, Hector was doing great.

Lieutenant Colonel Bolt usually seemed lost in deep thoughts. Today being no different. The probability of going into the Gulf and finding a valuable possession within an hour, even with a map, is incredible. Without a map and just random turns was astounding.

Since Subject 9's disappearance, Bolt had felt that things were different. This was a classic case of why they were monitoring him. People search decades for treasures around the Floridian waters, coming up empty-handed. If they could tap the power Subject 9 has, control, and refine it, the possibilities were endless.

Chapter 26

AMY'S QUESTION

Some days everything seems to fall perfectly into place, so another surprise occurred later that day. Amy had left a text message saying she wanting to talk. Brand responded with anytime! After her last visit, they had not talked, even after several texts from Brand. Though he had stopped talking to her, his feelings never stopped talking to him.

He missed a woman's ways. Sometimes that look from his first ex-wife saying, did I marry the stupidest man on the planet. Knowing it's crazy to miss something like that and still missing it are the conundrums of life.

Arrangements were made to meet at a steak house. They had eaten pizza the last time, and Brand's favorite meal was steak, so it seemed fair. Also, he was hoping for good news maybe coming his way and wanted everything to be perfect if that occurred. Really he had no idea what Amy's, "wanting to talk," was all about, but it never hurts to think positive. In that regard, one of Brand's favorite sayings is, "It's never too late for good news."

When he saw her again, for it had been a couple of months, she was even prettier than he remembered. Maybe his memory was being kind so as not to make him suffer without her beauty beside him. It was more than her beauty that attracted Brand to her.

Her hair was black and long, with her brown eyes and the cutest cheeks anyone should be allowed to have. She was wearing black leggings with a black top that had buckles, zippers and hooks. It look great on her. Amy was so much more than the clothes she wore.

She was like a deep lake that can look so peaceful on the surface, but you would never believe how deep it truly was. Amy could make almost anyone fall in love with her and had so many fans, yet never was ostentatious.

Brand started by giving a compliment, as was his nature when seeing almost anyone. It makes people feel good and cost nothing.

There were a few people he would insult to see if he could get a rise out of them, afterward letting them in on the joke. If Brand totally ignored you, that said something.

Before Brand could say anything, she rushed up and gave him another wonderful hug, the kind that only Amy can do. Brand never wanted Amy's hugs to end, after they parted, he started.

"Amy, how is it possible for you to get even prettier than the last time I saw you. Flowers cry when you enter the room their so jealous," stated Brand.

She gave the typical Amy look like thanks, but I don't believe you, but really thanks. Amy was like that, she could get along with just about everyone, and she had many different looks that said many different things.

The truth was, she really did look great, and seeing her in front of him brought a bit of pain that the memory thankfully allows us to forget.

Once they settled down to placing orders and getting drinks, Amy was ready to talk, but mostly listen. She was a great listener, which is very rare in these times.

Amy began, "My girlfriend and boyfriend both want to marry me. I don't understand why they can't just enjoy my time without trying to own me? I love them both," Then looking at Brand added, "And you know your special, but I just want things to stay as they are. You have a Zen about you, I want your peace-"

At that point, Brand had to interrupted, "You're not around me enough," with a big smile.

Amy continued, "Really older people seem more at peace. How do I get that without getting old?"

Now Brand could see that Amy was very serious and more than ready to listen.

Brand replied with a serious tone, "To find peace, you have to start with the inside. You have to forgive yourself for all the things you have failed at. Relations with parents, siblings, children, and friends. Once you have forgiven yourself, it is easy to forgive others for all they have done to you." And then he added with a big smile.

"When you have achieved that, call me up and tell me how to do it!" At that, Amy did not respond, and Brand could see she wanted more, so he continued.

"The next step is not to expect anything from anyone. I really enjoy your company but don't expect it often. So when you are with me, it is great, but I don't expect it to happen regularly, if really ever again. Enjoying the moment without the expectation it will come again."

At that moment, the food arrived and with a great meal at hand most talk ended till desserts arrived.

With the arrival of the desserts, the conversation had turned to Brand's new tattoo.

Amy asking, "I want to know where you got that tattoo? Why that design and why your arm? I have never seen one that looks so real, so fresh. When was it done?"

Brand with a cat's smile said, "If I tell you the truth, you won't believe me."

Amy answering "Try me!"

Brand continued, "It's not a tattoo. It's alive and speaks to me telepathically." Now he paused to really take in her expression. She still hadn't spoken.

"I, well we agree it would sit on my arm so I could make sure it would be safe." And as an afterthought continued, "Of course it does not need me to be safe."

Amy now spoke, "Why is it in the shape of a sword?" She asked with true curiosity like she believed all that was previously said.

Brand responded, "It can take any form it wants. I have always been impressed with the Romain soldiers. They used what is call a short sword, great weapon when your outnumbered. They also liked it because you were close when you killed your opponent. It read my mind and transformed into it."

Then Brand added, "I was in a fight to the death, and it help me to win. And yes, that is another story you probably won't believe."

Now Amy had that look in her eyes. It was a look that cannot be described. Then out of nowhere, she said.

"You should write a book."

At that, they both started laughing, to the point that people were staring. It was time to leave, and when you're with people you love, that time is always too soon.

They both, in their own way, had a deep affection for the other.

As they left the steak house Brand's iPhone went off with Joey on the other end. Whatever Joey was saying he was upset or nervous and it was loud and urgent.

Brand responded, "I understand, be right there."

Chapter 27

JINN TROUBLE

Now all his attention was with Joey. He knew this would happen, but lately, it had become hard to tell what may happen and what has happened. If only he could get a premonition regarding the lottery.

Luck is a funny thing. Sometimes the luckiest thing is not to be lucky!

Brand listened to the story Joey had told him on their boat trip a couple of days ago. After all the events Brand had just gone through, he was far less skeptical of Joey's story. He had much more concern for if it could be real.

Joey, by nature, was secretive, and being his last profession was a spy, he became obsessed with it. This explained the secret note given when a simple invitation to go boating would have sufficed.

Trying to get information out of Joey was always on a need-to-know basis at best. Trying to find out where the bottle originated containing the Jinn was futile. Brand tried to explain that all the information he could collect would help in providing a solution to Joey's current problem, but all he would get is that look.

Brand could only imagine his friend's struggles. Deep down, who would give up a bottle containing a Jinn? With a prize like that, the sky is the limit. Granted, Joey was well off, he still wasn't in that class where price does not matter.

On the boat, Joey explained that he was sure there was a Jinn inside that could perform feats not imagined possible. He also explained that given the correct wording in his wish he could get his son back alive and well. Knowing Brand's tenacity for getting positive results, Joey wanted his help with the wording.

That was when Brand told him to forget the idea and wish for something else. Anything that did not involve the dead.

The next day is when Joey met with Brand again. This time coming to Brand's rig. He still wanted help with the wording to bring his dead son back to life. Again, Brand denied his request even though deep-down, he knew Joey would try it anyway.

Maybe Brand wanted to have clean hands when it all would go wrong. Playing around with life and death is always bad. If you're alive, you may end up dead, and if dead, God forbid you become alive.

Now the worst had happened, and Joey's dead son Bill was a zombie looking to eat fresh meat and drink blood. Maybe zombie is the wrong word, but whatever the right word was, it was an abomination.

Joey did have the sense to at least contain him with a chain attached tightly to his waist locked via padlock and secured by four bolted plates hooked to the cement floor. There were about 6 feet of movement that the chain allowed.

In the spy business, you always have a plan B. Joey must have had doubts, and thankfully he had made arrangements in case things went bad.

Brand was surveying the situation. He looked directly into Joey's eyes and commanded, "Give me the bottle with the Jinn, now!" It was not a request but an order. People in the military know the difference.

Joey had always been in charge during their missions together. He was not used to taking orders from someone like Brand, but he had asked for his help. Now Brand was in charge.

Joey did not answer for many long seconds and finally said, "It will take 15 minutes."

Wherever Joey hid it, Brand knew without Joey's help, it would not be found. When dealing with certain people, you have to know their strengths and weaknesses. Joey was a professional in hiding things and keeping secrets.

It was a long 15 minutes until Joey came back with an old-looking bottle that you would imagine in an Arabian movie. It was about 4 inches wide, having an oval-shaped bottom with sides forming a larger oval. It was about 7 inches wide and 6 inches tall, not counting the plug on top. The front had ornate carvings of what appeared to be branches with leaves. The stopper was plain, being a plug securing the inside contents.

Joey handed the bottle to Brand, and with that, Brand said, "Don't do anything. I want to do research and will figure something out." That too was an order which was understood accordingly by both men.

Then Brand stated, "I will call you soon."

Brand realized there was not much time to resolve this before it would get really out of hand. The most important thing currently was to keep Bill securely contained until he could figure a way of killing him. At the same time making sure Joey would not kill him for re-killing his dead son. Brand was not taking anything for granted in regards to what Joey could or would do.

Lieutenant Colonel Bolt had been monitoring Brand's audio from his phone and was extremely concerned on what next to do. This was a national security event, and if it got out of hand, everything could be in jeopardy. He would have to push this up the chain, which he hated to do.

Keeping control means not having to call for help or advice. But this was different. The United States government is big, and there were professional teams to handle these types of situations. He was not rushing to make the call.

Chapter 28

TIME FOR A PLAN

Brand was now driving home with the Jinn's bottle, trying to figure out how to resolve Joey's problem.

With all this going on, Amy was on his mind. She looked more beautiful than the last time. There are some people that you naturally feel wonderful with.

Not wanting to be honest with himself, he knew he still hoped for one final woman in his life. Not just any woman but someone really special. He had let himself hope that might be Amy. People like that are loved by many, and their kindness can lead to misunderstandings. She has a specialness that so few others have. Sometimes dreams are all you can have.

The truth is, Joey's problem was pressing, and he would have to put his full attention to its resolution if he wanted to have any dreams at all. His intuition was telling him time was of the essence, so once he arrived home, he needed to devise a plan.

Usually, he would contact Darrell to get information regarding something unusual. As he gathered information from the net, he now realized why. There were many different versions of the Jinn or Genie. How could he decide which one was correct? Some were providing one wish while others giving three. Time was against him. The feeling was like every minute that passed by moved him closer to failure.

Joey would only be able to contain his dead now alive son Bill for so long. Brand was worried that Joey would either lose containment or his life, or both.

Brand's brain raced through the different scenarios. Each taking too much time or not providing any substantial benefit compared to the current situation. The obvious answer came to him.

He would open the bottle and ask the Jinn what he can and can not do. Asking a question was not a wish. Once he knew how many wishes he would have and any limitations, then he could make his plans.

Deep down, he already was hoping for more than one wish. Funny, he never asked Joey how many he had. Many different thoughts went in and out of Brand's mind.

Brand set up his iPhone to record the event, knowing Bubba would make big money if the video came out well. Also, he wanted proof given that the past paranormal events that had happened, the demon, vampire, and aliens, there had been no video or any real evidence of their existence or that anything had really happened. The haunted house was destroyed, and only the ground supporting it remained. The sandpit with Gabriel was filled in, and no remains of its existence was evident. The aliens were very good at covering their operations. At least now he was ready and prepared to prove this really happened.

The cap to the bottle came off easily, so easily it was surprising. It did not fall off anytime it was moved. Once he removed the cap, the bottle itself seemed to heat up.

At the same time, an orange mist appeared, gaining density quickly in size and structure. Most people would have dropped the bottle at that point or earlier, but Brand was trained somewhat for things like this, the unexpected happening while still keeping your senses.

He had slowly and carefully set the bottle down while it was starting to feel hot. The actual hot feeling ending quickly, even before he had set it standing up on the table. The orange mist grew in form until it was human size and forming a solid shape.

Brand expected the Jinn type from the Arabian literature, but what came out was the TV show, "I Dream of Genie" kind.

She was gorgeous. Seemingly based on his first love, she had brownish and blondish hair with tones of light to medium orange highlights going down past her shoulders, ending at the middle of her back. Her big blue eyes were complimented with red lips that were full and perfectly proportioned to each other. Her skin tone was white with a little color, leaning towards pale tones but was perfect to her countenance.

She wore tight blue jeans with a black T-shirt tucked into her pants sporting a cobra insignia on the front. By this point, she was fully formed and would seem like any beautiful young woman you would be lucky to meet.

Looking at Brand with the sweetest smile, she said, "Master, what is your wish?"

Brand was taken back. Whatever he expected, it was not this. She made the atmosphere extremely disarming, and he had to be more conscious of his words being in such a relaxed state.

Brand replied, "I have questions regarding my wishes, but I don't want my questions to count as a wish."

The Jinn looked amused and replied with, "That is not a problem, but you only have one wish, Master."

Brand was greatly disappointed with that news. He was hoping for three and at least to use one for his own benefit.

He continued, "Is there anything you cannot do?" "Like rules that cannot be broken?"

Now the Jinn who looked amused before changed into a more serious but still very friendly manner.

She replied, "Oh, there are, but far too many to speak. If you tell me what your wish will be, I can answer if possible or not."

Brand was still disappointed he had only one wish. If he had three, one would be to undo what Joey had done, but the other two wishes would have been his. So many desires, but even just one more wish would change his life forever.

Brand asked, "Can I undo a wish by someone else?"

Now the Jinn had a curious look and stated that another's wish cannot be revoked.

She was looking into Brand's eyes and asked, "Master, what is it *you* truly desire? I suggest you think about what will make you happy and not worry about fixing someone else's problem."

It seemed like the Jinn could not only see into Brand's heart but also his thoughts.

On the one hand he would not even have a wish to make if not for Joey giving him the Jinn's bottle. So, trying to fix Joey's problem felt only right. But on the other hand, he could make his life so much better even with just one wish. This opportunity will never come again, and he really needed to think about what one wish he really wanted. The Jinn was right. He needed to focus on what *he* really wanted.

At this point, Brand was fighting an internal conflict where whichever side wins, he would be a loser. What he really needed was more time to think. Deep down, he felt time was working against him. The longer it took to resolve this the greater chance it would get worse.

The thought of having even one wish granted could make such a huge difference in his life. He could find true love or have a fortune or maybe both. Then again, he could speak, read and understand all languages, which had always been something Brand wanted to do since he was a child. There were so many things like extending his life. Or looking and feeling again like 25 years old. His mind kept going into all different scenarios, and then it hit him.

Mary had told him he would fix her brother Tommy. And she was right, he just had to word his wish correctly. There is a big difference between bringing back the dead and wishing away a little boy's cancer.

It's amazing how when a big decision is made everything else just falls into place. He knew they were taking him to St. Jude Children's Research Hospital. It amazed him on how hard it must be to do and how strong and brave those who provide that type of work. They set up a hospital for children with severe illnesses. Their families are charged nothing and provided lodging nearby at no cost.

At that, he felt good, and isn't that the purpose of a wish? To feel good afterward with no guilt or second thoughts.

With that finally settled in his mind, the problem of Joey's son, Bill, now would be addressed. Maybe with cement and a deep hole on the same abandoned farm that Gabriel Hand perished at would work. Put Bill into a container and fill it with cement and bury it deep with cement on top. Especially if the place was abandoned and it was deep enough.

Now the hard part would be to sell the idea to Joey! It felt like it might work, and at least having a chance of success picked up his spirits and energy.

Lieutenant Colonel Bolt knew he had to make the call being this could possibly become a national security event. For some reason Subject 9's phone was not transmitting audio or video for that matter. He hated to have to make the call. The biggest was the lack of control. With his call, there goes his authority.

The personnel trained for such events do not discriminate killing the good with the bad. Their main focus is containment and cleanup, with speed being a high priority.

Bolt had some unreasonable faith that Subject 9 would resolve this without much help needed or just Bolt's resources being used. Bolt pondered many things but, in the end, knew he would make the call shortly.

Chapter 29

SPY WORK

In the spy business, everyone is betraying someone. The person who is your best friend or even lover may not be who you believe they are. And at some point, they will show their hand usually when you need them the most.

Brand was working on adrenaline or maybe just the excitement of a new event that often happens in one's youth but becomes rarer as age sets in. He contacted Joey and told him he was coming over to resolve the problem.

Brand got onto Matilda and was ready to go when Roy appeared, asking where he was going and if he needed any help. It was unusual for Roy to inquire into Brand's life, especially at the moment something important was happening.

Things like that always attracted his attention, human nature. This was not human nature for Roy to do.

He declined the offer of help and said, "Just feel like riding my girl Matilda," as he sped off to the main gate in the night's total blackness.

Lieutenant Colonel Bolt made the call to an advisor of the President, Sam Smith, who thanked him, stating it would be handled. Bolt was thinking, so this is how retirement will be. He would rather have it end on the field of battle. That helpless feeling like the world plays its hand and you're not even in the game. It was an unusual feeling for Bolt, but worse, he felt like he let Subject 9 down.

Darrell Green had secretly installed monitoring software on Subject 9's phone. He was monitoring the phone and knew about the Jinn.

Even though Subject 9's phone went offline, it was now back online with full monitoring capabilities.

He had also installed a tracking device onto Subject 9's bike and knew he was going back to Joey's house.

Knowing this would be his only opportunity to gain freedom from both Bolt and Subject 9. He thought about spies and their handlers. They think they are so smart and tough. He will show them how unspecial they really are. Darrell's talent in retrieving information and his research capabilities made him believe he not only was their equal but their superior.

Now was the time. He had already written down a wish that would secure him and his family's future while also providing them protection from people like Bolt. Once his wish was granted, everything would change to the best life possible. But timing is everything, and he had to make his move now before Brand gets onto Joey's property.

Joey's home was not large, but it was nice, having a beautiful backyard and was secluded. Of course, that is relative compared to Brand's rig on the farm. Joey's neighbors were a couple of miles away on each sides, plus front and back. It had a long driveway with a type of guardhouse at the beginning, with the home resting at the end. There were no street lights making only the moon's illumination plus the gate's lights the only source to view the surroundings.

Matilda was never quiet, making Brand's entrance always an announcement. Brand's senses were on high alert, not really knowing how Joey would react when he found out the truth.

But there was more than that going on, like a spider's sense of imminent danger. The same feeling he had while under the water treasure hunting with Bubba.

That is when Darrell appeared out of the darkness, in front and from the right. He was coming straight to Brand walking quickly and stopping about 4 feet between the two men.

There was an intense silence, one man holding a bottle and the other a gun. One nervous and the other angry but calm.

The nervous man holding the gun started with, "Give me the bottle."

Brand seemed not to even hear Darrell, like he was deep in thought and then.

"Darrell, GO HOME." Brand had an ability to make people do what he desired and, at that moment, was putting all his energy into trying to make that happen.

Darrell's response was, "I will kill you and take it. Why not just put it down and walk away."

Brand, anger now showing through, "You're playing a game you don't know how to play. You have never been in the field. You don't know the rules. Go home to your wife and children."

Now Darrell's outrage kicked in with his response.

"You, Bolt, you all think you're so tough and smart. I am holding the gun, and you have underestimated me."

Brand's responded, "You don't even know if I am holding a gun or not. Have you checked both my hands? Knowing that now Darrell would check his hands, Brand continued.

"If I were really playing, I would kill you without a thought, but I will not hurt you. Darrell, please go home! Think of your wife and children. Please go home, and this NEVER happened."

Darrell now was ready to kill Brand. You can see it in a man's eyes when he has had enough. Darrell giving his last statement, "Give me the bottle or I shoot."

There are some distinct sounds. The sound of glass breaking or nails scratching a blackboard. The sound of a silencer is truly distinct. Brand heard it, but Darrell never did. The first shot went through his ear with the second shot an inch above that. Both shots were fired in succession, with not even a full second in between.

Darrell went down fast and hard. One moment a live human being and the next just dead. Like he had no meaning or value, just something that needed to be taken care of.

Brand was furious. Joey had appeared from the guardhouse and had a smile saying, "No need to thank me."

Brand's anger was released with, "None given! Why did you do that? I had it under control. That man had a wife and children!

Joey reacting more to Brand's anger than his words, "My old friend, he had a gun and was going to kill you. I thought I was helping!"

Brand understood Joey and his words. But he wanted no more blood on his hands. He had vowed no more violence and then there was the Tiny incident. Now Darrell's greed cost him his life. And yet Brand still felt he was in ways responsible. Still, there was the mission at hand, and he had to stay focused.

There are times when you can feel the electricity in the air, when the outcome of an event is shrouded in mystery. Especially whether you will walk away or never walk again. Moments like this are what life is truly about, the rest of the time is just waiting.

They walked into the backyard, which had most of the lights turned off. It was then that Brand saw Joey had an associate waiting for them. He was a young man but meticulous in his attire, down to his personal appearance. Brand's instincts were saying he was an assassin. Joey did not introduce him, but the young man's eyes never left Brand.

Joey was walking in front of Brand, and after Brand saw his accomplice, he stopped walking. Joey continued until he was next to the assassin. There were about 6 feet between them and Brand.

This moment was going to be intense, but Brand was not expecting what happened next.

The government team sent were experts at what they do. This consisted in terminations, extractions, recoveries, and containment. Like the great warriors of the past, the determining factor in their successes was great training, allowing them to work as a team. In this case, there were not eight soldiers but one who could do eight things while being able to rearrange his resources as quickly as needed. Like the great Roman army, many working as a unit can beat incredible odds.

Lieutenant Colonel Bolt sat feeling helpless and, for the first time, started to doubt his decision. For a warrior, that is not allowed. You need your senses focused on the current situation for the best possible outcome. There is no room for regrets or doubts.

Joey who was looking into Brand's eyes said, "You already made a wish, didn't you?" It was said with a cold tone, like it had already been calculated with the answer known before it was said.

Brand was not in a defensive mood when he responded, "I tried to help, but you would not listen. I am still trying to help."

Joey had a cold look with a stare Brand had never seen him have before. He asked, "So what did you wish for?" But before Brand could answer, he added, "And you still came here with the Jinn. Were you thinking that I would say okay, no problem?"

Brand responded, "The Jinn delights in making wishes fail. Look what happened to your son Bill. After much thought, I wished for Tommy, a little boy who has cancer, a total recovery."

At this point, Joey could not contain himself and said, "You were always lucky, but the talk was you were smart. So, you're telling me you did not wish for anything for yourself?"

Brand's answer being, "That's the point. If I had, she would have ruined it. I figure a righteous wish can't go wrong."

What he did not say was he was not going to give Joey a second chance in regards to his now zombie son.

Joey was no longer himself. He was now someone that Brand did not know. When some men are on a mission, they will let nothing stop them.

Joey, with a cold stare and voice, said, "I expected you to fail me. That's why he is here now," referring to the young man next to him. "You can give me the bottle, or it will be taken from your dead body!"

Then the Joey Brand knew said as an explanation with a pleading undertone, "You have two kids, you must understand!"

Brand had expected to see the assassin's gun but not the one Joey was pointing at him. With two guns pointed at him from 6 feet in semi-darkness, he might make it out alive if he resisted, but the better odds were in just doing whatever Joey wanted and being allowed to leave.

Joey and Brand lived by different rules than most, and no matter how bad a situation became many times, you could still just walk away.

Where someone with less spy experience might panic, they would not. This was just a game where Joey wanted to make sure "his" Jinn was returned. Once that happened, Brand would be set free.

The problem was the Jinn was no longer attached to that bottle. The way Brand saw it, you don't give a drunk monkey a machine gun, period. Once he had the Jinn, he was never going to return it to Joey. Look at what had already happened. We now have a zombie Bill to deal with.

But once Joey finds out he has been tricked, then there will be trouble.

Brand started to say, "It won't..." but before he could finish, there were two bright red laser lights, one on Joey's forehead and the other on the assassin's forehead right between their eyes. Each looked at the other before Joey looked back at Brand.

Joey's eyes were saying, you betrayed me, but if he was in his right mind, he would have seen the surprise in Brand's eyes.

There is a look when even the most contained person will show surprise if the surprise is big enough.

Then before either spoke, a voice seemed to be projected right between them even though no one was there.

The voice stated, "PUT DOWN YOUR WEAPONS, NOW!" That part seemed to startle Brand because it was really odd the way the sound emanated from between them with no one there. Obviously, it was sound projection, but he never realized it could be so good.

Now everything seemed to slow down for Brand. A second become a minute. It was like watching slow-motion replay but with a clarity that was sharper.

At that moment, zombie Bill came crashing through the patio glass door. His attention was on Joey, and he was heading straight for him. This is where Brand's slow-motion started, where no one moved except for Joey by turning to his left where zombie Bill was coming from. The laser light was off him, and he then fired two rounds into Zombie Bill's chest, which barely slowed him down.

Then Joey, who still was the only one moving except for Zombie Bill, put a third-round right between Zombie Bill's eyes while falling backward to the ground, but that only slowed the thing down for a moment. It was then that others started to react. The entire event was probably three seconds but felt much longer to Brand.

Then many things seemed to happen at once. The assassin was shot between the eyes while Brand, who only had the empty Jinn bottle in his hand, was pushed back and contained by two agents away from the new scene about to unfold.

At the same time, Brand was pushed back and Joey's friend was shot, Joey was disarmed of his weapon by two agents and also pulled away from the area they were all at. Then within another second, there were four men wearing what looked like full hazmat suits with large tanks on their backs.

The hazmat men began spraying a thick amber color jelly-like substance that seemed cold, or at least that was the sensation Brand was feeling while watching the event occur. That immediately slowed zombie Bill down to almost no movement at all. Once zombie Bill was completely covered with the amber substance, they then began spraying a dark grey mist which seemed to react with the amber color substance turning it a dark purple. Brand had the feeling that this was hardening the amber substance like cement when it sets.

The whole process was maybe five minutes long, but it seemed shorter than that to Brand. Then the cleanup and fake stories were created to explain away all that had happened. This time the "whitey" light did not work on Brand, and he faked its effects.

The story they told Joey was that he had become drunk, called Brand, went to bed, and had a bad dream believing his dead son was alive. It was such a bad dream he ran outside through the patio glass door. It was suggested he stop drinking. Brand had arrived and helped him back to his bed before leaving. Then a cleanup crew, which usually follows the former group, cleaned up as much as they could, including inside his home, and left Joey in his bedroom with the fake memories implanted inside Joey's consciousness.

There must be other memories that would signal to Joey all is not right, but obviously, he was still important to them so his life could continue.

When spies die, sometimes the equilibrium is upset by actions that happen after they pass. The powers in control will allow certain people to live because it keeps the balance in check.

In Brand's case, they tried to implant memories that Joey had called him needing help, and when he arrived, he saw Joey on the lawn drunk. He helped Joey get back in his home and into bed and then went back home himself to a great night's sleep.

After Brand viewed the light, it had no effect, and it was just an agent telling him a story he was supposed to think really happened. He was aware of everything during the whole process. This reminded him of the demon he met in that abandoned farmhouse.

Brand's mind was unraveling a giant knot, and, in that regard, he started to see the bigger picture of how so many things were tied together.

Before Darrell's death, he mentioned the name Bolt. Even though Brand had no knowledge of this person, they were connected, and this man Bolt was important. Another lead to unravel.

Brand had no idea where they moved zombie Bill but was able to see that they picked him up and put him in a thick plastic-rubber body bag. He seemed like he was in a frozen state and provided no resistance.

Roy was now there with his truck and trailer to transport Brand back to the farm. Roy strapped down Matilda onto the trailer and put Brand in the passenger seat of the truck.

Brand was faking the dream state that he observed Joey in with no one being aware of his deception. His mind, though, was anything but in a dream state. So many little things now made sense. Each little thing was becoming a part of something much bigger. It felt like he now was awake for the first time in a long while. It would take time to sort it out, but changes had to be made in his future.

Chapter 30

ANSWERS

The bottle that Brand had was confiscated by the government team, but it was no use to them now. The Jinn and Brand had a long talk before he made his wish, and she moved to the crystal skull he had just recently found.

She explained that the source, meaning vessel where they, the Jinn, reside, is like a phone number being called to them. They do not really live in a bottle but can instantly come forth when being called from a source they are attached to in this plane of existence.

She also explained to his disappointment that she did not allow his phone to record her image or sounds as they like to remain anonymous, but she did put one picture of herself within his phone as a gift because she liked him or, as she put it, "You're special Master."

She explained that so many wishes are for one's own personal gain that they are always tainted with failure. The bigger the greed, the greater it will not go well. Playing around with life after death is not for this world and was destined for disaster.

He could still hear her say, "But your wish Master was of noble design. It is a rare thing and must be granted with no ill side effects."

They talked about many things, then she left him as if she was never there. It had felt so good to be in her company that he had forgotten she was a Jinn, but now in an instant, he was alone. It occurred so fast that for a moment, he felt like he must have dreamed the entire event.

Brand would say that there is a sound that can be heard when there are no sounds at all. It is like a hum that, once heard, can never be unheard. It only occurs when it is absolutely silent. Then it can be heard so loud it can make you crazy.

Roy had taken him home and put him into his rig stretched out on his bed. Sweetbull was, of course, happy to see him, and Brand could tell Sweetbull knew he was faking his trance state.

As he sat there that night, his head would not stop thinking about this or that. The first thought was of Darrell. There are mistakes made like the Tiny incident. At least though Tiny is still alive, and then there are the tragedies like Darrell. A good man but greed and delusion of superiority created his demise. Still, Brand felt bad, wondering how he could have prevented the event from happening.

The Tiny fight still was bothering him, but he heard and felt no blowback from it.

Then there was Amy. He never dared tell her how much he truly liked her. And when she didn't answer his texts, that hurt. Though when together, she felt so right. Like a very complex puzzle that has two pieces with a lot of angles. Together they made one beautiful picture.

Then his thoughts went to past events.

Darrell had always been so helpful, and Roy was always there when needed. The help with the demon that would have surely killed him if there had been no intervention. The pit that was so carefully constructed and worked so well in killing Gabriel Hand. Now this night with Joey, obviously someone is protecting him, but exactly who and why was yet to be determined.

Maybe Darrell's last words, Bolt was the answer.

Brand decided the best course of action would be to get some good sleep. When that happens, everything looks different and better. Answers just seemed to come to problems.

The next morning was beautiful, even by Floridian standards. Brand received a phone call from Joey, who seemed mentally confused but thanked him for his help and mentioned he was going to slow down on the drinking.

As the morning was settling into the afternoon, Brand remembered the Jinn said she would provide a picture of herself. He looked within the pictures on his iPhone, and it was as she had stated.

The picture consisted of a beautiful young woman in a black dress wearing a tulle skirt rising up to her breasts then stopping and displaying her bare shoulders. She was slightly turned with one arm bent, leaving her hand resting on her hip. Her red lips and golden orange hair was flowing on each side of her enchanting face. With an expression that is hard to describe, saying, "This is for you!" But really, there was so much more in that look unsaid.

She was in front of a forest which was slightly blurred out, having a thick orange mist behind her.

The picture looked professionally created, and Brand was surprised she would provide that type of photo. Of course, it just looked like a beautiful woman in a forest filled with an orange mist. No one would believe that it was a Jinn!

To Brand, it was priceless. She was amazing, and the picture just reconfirmed that. Having it did make him feel special as he imagined all the wishes she had performed and how no one else ever had received her image. She had been so sweet to him and complied in answering all his questions, which she did not have to do.

The truth is, he felt he was special to her, and that really made him feel great. But like all double-edged swords, he missed her already and knew that would never go away and certainly at times be much worse.

Bubba left a text saying, "Buddy, I am taking you to lunch. I have big news."

Hector was busy most of the time, but he and his girl were moving up. They now had a nice home. More importantly, they really loved each other. It was beautiful to see that. Brand missed his company but was happy for his future.

Having a partner and gaining wealth is the very best when it happens together.

Lieutenant Colonel Bolt was not pleased with the outcome concerning Joey and Subject 9. To him, the team missed the most important thing, the Jinn. Yes, they had the bottle, which was useless. Now it was nothing more than an old Arabian-style bottle with a loose cap. Subject 9 must have the Jinn and transferred the contents to another container. That container needed to be found and acquired.

After lunch with Bubba, Brand headed back to Roy's farm, where Sweetbull was waiting for his return. She hated him leaving and always looked like it was the last time they would see each other when he departed.

Even after the great lunch and company of Bubba, Brand was in a depressed mood. He missed having a special woman in his life. His first ex-wife, well, that was a lost cause. It was Amy that bothered him. She would have really been perfect.

Slipping into a melancholy state sitting outside, Sweetbull ran up with a weathered inch thick rope. The rope having been through many battles between two friends. She shoved it into Brand's lap, saying, "Daddy, it's time to play," and of course, she was right.

Chapter 31

Epilogue DRAGONFLY

Sam Smith was not elected by the people, yet he had a higher security access than the President. He was not known to the public or most people for that matter, the exceptions being only the highest in commands. Having incredible power and still being anonymous is the mark of a wise man. Whether Republicans or Democrats, his title always remained the same, advisor to the President.

People like politicians come and go. Sam Smith always remained in power. It was said you would not see his hand, but you will feel it. Most could not tell you what he looked like or sounded. That was part of his power over people. Like the boogeyman unseen until it is too late.

To the few that dealt with him, he was short with words and always business. That is why the poor soul, now who had to give him the bad news of what just occurred, was worried about being the messenger.

The work they do is never published. For if the public knew about their work, which was combining multiple animal genetic materials together while also creating a new unique genetic code with all the combined traits of each animal mixed, that would surely create a huge outcry from all directions.

Their work was always done in secret, providing the ability to use fewer safety protocols with speed of completion always being important. There were accidents along the process, but in science, that element is always there.

Occasionally an accident brings incredible results that, because of the situation, cannot be replicated. The net result a truly unique being.

Dragonfly was that incredible accident.

The building was plain-looking, having one story with a flat roof and brick skin. No windows with a very small parking lot. Most would pass it by without a second look or thought.

Unlike its one floor on the surface, it descended down, having six basement floors. Each floor having higher security procedures and, what few personnel were there, less access to them.

Once entering the building, the first thing that seemed odd was the short hallway to another set of doors that were much more reinforced than the doors off the street. The main purpose of this floor was just to process the small number of personnel that entered and left the building.

Dean was in charge of security at the building, working there for over a decade. When working that long in a facility with such high security, he was always a bit paranoid while keeping his thoughts to himself.

His inner thoughts abhorred the place and his job. He was really a prison warden with very few prisoners. And because Dean was human, at some point started to feel sorry for whatever crimes they had committed. In this case, the crime was being created.

They only had one prisoner on the sixth floor. Between her beauty and brains plus special abilities and disposition, she had to be contained, but still, at some level, Dean had pity for her. The life she was born to and now lives were sad.

Dean's inner thoughts were, she should have never been able to be created, never been able to grow and survive. Yet through luck and maybe her own will she was perfect...except for her hatred for humans. Not just a hatred but having extreme homicidal tendencies when around any humans. That was Dragonfly.

Sam Smith answered his phone as he always did with, "Yes." The agent on the other end identified himself, even though he knew Sam knew who it was, and proceeded with the following.

"Dragonfly has broken containment. She left a two-word message. It's a name, Brand Wright."

Sam now asked one question with one word.

"Connection?"

"He was the agent that put her into containment the last time she was active. We believe she will locate and finalize him. What would you like done, sir?"

To Be Continued

About the Author

Brad lives in Bradenton, Florida, with his pit bull Raine enjoying semi-retirement. Bshprintz@mac.com

Author's Notes:

Thank you, Jason Shprintz, for your editing and help with plot development. Jason is my son who has won awards for his writing abilities. He currently has published *The Reverie,* which can be purchased on Amazon.

Thank you, Jennifer Shprintz, my daughter, for your help with plot development and doing the work of uploading the manuscript, front and back covers, so this book could be published.

Special thank you to Brittany Wilson, who created SUBJECT 9 book cover, spine, and back cover. She is wonderful to work with, and her talent speaks for itself. Thank you for your art and help in bringing my ideas to life in a way I could not imagine! She can be contacted at https://www.brittwilsonart.com/book-cover-design

And most importantly, thank you, the reader, who has spent the time and hopefully enjoyed this book of fun tales with deeper meanings. I truly appreciate you!